Disney
Cruella

Published by Scholastic Australia in 2021.

Scholastic Australia Pty Limited
PO Box 579 Gosford NSW 2250
ABN 11 000 614 577
www.scholastic.com.au

Part of the Scholastic Group
Sydney · Auckland · New York · Toronto · London · Mexico City
New Delhi · Hong Kong · Buenos Aires · Puerto Rico

NATIONAL LIBRARY OF AUSTRALIA
A catalogue record for this book is available from the National Library of Australia

ISBN 978-1-76112-624-6

Printed by McPherson's Printing Group, Maryborough, VIC.

10 9 8 7 6 5 4 3 2 1 21 22 23 24 25 / 2

Disney Cruella

Adapted by Elizabeth Rudnick
Screenplay by Dana Fox and Tony McNamara
Story by Aline Brosh McKenna and
Kelly Marcel & Steve Zissis
Based upon the Novel "The One Hundred
and One Dalmatians" by Dodie Smith
Based on Disney's *Cruella*

SCHOLASTIC
SYDNEY AUCKLAND NEW YORK TORONTO LONDON MEXICO CITY
NEW DELHI HONG KONG BUENOS AIRES PUERTO RICO

To the staff and students at CCLCS, who every day teach and learn the importance of being true to yourself

"What sets you apart can sometimes feel like a burden, and it's not. And a lot of the time, it's what makes you great."

—*Emma Stone*

PROLOGUE

Cruella De Vil wasn't born. She was made. Although, if we are being technical, she was, in truth, like any living, breathing being, born. Her name was Estella. And it is rumored that on the night of her birth, the stars didn't shine and the moon dared not peek out from behind the stormy clouds. Some say that wolves howled, and others say the rivers around her home ran hot.

But people say a lot of things.

And a lot of the time, those things are not true.

At least not all of them.

Estella came into the world like any other baby–kicking and screaming. But from the moment she arrived, it was clear that she was not like any other baby. Unique, some called her. Special, said others. A few kinder souls who came across her rolling along in her pram might have even dared call her cute–until her knit cap fell off, revealing her hair.

Jet black on one side, pure white on the other. It was, from the moment she was born, thick and distinct. And when people saw it, they usually stopped thinking *cute* and started thinking *bizarre*.

But mothers are blinded by love and Estella's mother, Catherine, was no exception. To Catherine, Estella was perfect and brilliant from the moment she entered the world. As the days and years passed, Estella grew from a curious baby who was quick to smile, to a precocious toddler who insisted on doing everything on her own. She walked before other children her age and by two was having full conversations with her mum. She never seemed to notice the strange looks people gave her and never seemed bothered that no one came to visit the shabby but cozy cottage where she and her mother lived.

To Estella, her tiny home wasn't drab or sad. The clothes her seamstress mother mended brightened the small space and became her world. She slipped silk, chiffon, and taffeta through her fingers, marveling at their smoothness. She compared clothes and dreamed up patterns. As Estella grew older, other talents began to shine through. At her mother's knee, Estella quickly learned how to thread a needle and soon was darning socks and hemming skirts. When the meager furniture at home became too threadbare, Estella would create colorful patches out of fabric remnants.

While sewing came naturally to Estella, following the rules was a bit harder for her. On more than one occasion, Estella's mother had to give her a gentle reminder. "You must follow the pattern," she said to her daughter. "There's a way to do things."

"It's ugly," Estella said, holding up a pattern and comparing its straight lines to the wild ones she had imagined for her doll's new dress.

Her mother shook her head. "That's cruel. Your name is Estella, not Cruella."

Cruella was the nickname her mother had given her when she was younger and in the throes of the "terrible twos", which were followed by the "tyrannical threes". Estella's temper, when it got the best of her, could make her quite cranky and sometimes even mean. Her mother liked to remind her to keep "Cruella" in check–though some moments were easier than others. Sometimes, at the reminder, young Estella shook her head or–if in a particularly pouty mood–ripped up a pattern or stomped her feet. But she always returned to give her mother a hug and a "sorry". She didn't want to be cruel. She just wanted to sew.

By the time she was twelve years old, Estella was a talented seamstress. While she still didn't have many friends, her mother told her every day she was special. "You can be anybody or anything you want, sweet girl," her mum said. "You aren't just black or white. You're every color of the rainbow." And Estella believed her. Estella didn't need friends. She had her mum and her imagination.

So for the most part Estella was happy.

But all that was about to change . . .

Chapter 1

Twelve-year-old Estella sat astride her bicycle and stared up at the huge stone building in front of her that exuded wealth and privilege. The day she had been waiting for, well, forever was finally here.

She was going to start at a fancy private school. And while she was a little excited, she was also a lot terrified. Estella stared up at the building, absently rubbing the lining of her jacket, comforted by the feel of the fabric. She smiled. Maybe the school was like her jacket: it looked one way on the outside but was something entirely different on the inside.

She sighed.

She doubted it.

Kids began to stream into the courtyard seemingly from all directions, their uniforms immaculate and pressed perfectly. A row of fancy cars lined up, waiting to drop off more students. She heard shrieks of laughter as girls who hadn't seen each other over the holiday were reunited, and the deeper voices of the boys as they made their own, more reserved greetings. It all sounded like a foreign language to Estella.

She turned and looked at her mother, who was perched on a bicycle beside her. The woman's graying hair seemed to be forever attempting to escape its tilting bun, and the dull smock she wore was perpetually stained. She looked nothing like the women waving goodbye to their children from the windows of their cars. Every hair on those women's heads was perfectly smooth; their makeup was flawless and not a button was out of place. An unfamiliar sensation washed over Estella: looking at her mother, she was almost embarrassed.

"Remember," her mother said, interrupting Estella's thoughts, "you belong here as much as anybody."

Shame immediately washed over Estella. There she was, feeling self-conscious about her mother when all her mother had done for years was scrimp and save so that Estella could go to this silly school.

Taking a deep breath, Estella loosened her grip on the handlebars of her bike. She might not have gone to school with these kids before, but she wasn't going to let them bring her down–or at least she wasn't going to let her mother think they were getting to her. "Agreed," she said, her confident tone belying the doubt she was feeling.

Her mum nodded. "And what do you say to Cruella when she tries to get the better of you?"

Estella sighed. She hated that her mum still used that nickname for her slightly "wicked" side. But her mum wasn't wrong to remind her. She had to hold tight to her temper. "Thank you for coming, but you may go now," she recited dutifully.

Pleased by the answer, her mum gave her a small smile. Then she looked back and forth between the big, imposing building and Estella, her eyes distant. Estella wondered where her mother's thoughts had gone. There was something haunted–and deeply sad–in her expression.

Estella turned and looked at a group of girls in their matching uniforms, with hats tipped jauntily on their heads. She wore the same plain, ugly jacket and matching skirt they did–with a few small tweaks her mum didn't know about, of course. But she wasn't wearing the hat. Ever.

Taking a deep breath, Estella said one more goodbye to her mum, parked her bicycle in one of the racks, and joined the stream of students entering the school. When she reached the top of the steps, she turned around. Her mum was still there, watching. Estella gave her another wave and then turned and entered the building.

As soon as she was out of sight of her mum, Estella took her jacket off. Flipping it inside out, she smiled. The drab and itchy blue plaid was replaced by silk Estella had dyed a vibrant yellow. It was loud and jarring.

It was perfect.

Estella put the jacket back on and ran a hand through her hair. A surge of confidence rushed through her. She always felt better when rocking her own designs.

CHAPTER ONE

Ignoring the looks of the other students, some of whom had stopped and were blatantly staring, mouths open, Estella began to weave a path through the hallway. Even in the dim lighting, the jacket shone. Estella was proud of herself. She had spent hours, late at night, creating it. She had worked to blend the perfect dye and collected the silk piece by small piece from her mum's sewing jobs so she wouldn't know. The result was something unique and utterly *her*. Of course, that didn't mean everyone would understand. The other students weren't used to anyone stepping out of line. You wore the uniforms and followed the rules. But Estella had never been particularly great at following the rules.

Suddenly, two boys stepped in front of Estella. Stopping, she looked up at them, her face impassive. One of the boys had a mop of ginger hair and a mean expression. The other had cruel-looking eyes to go with his own equally unpleasant expression. Estella's mother had raised her to be kind–always. So Estella did what she figured any nice person would do: she introduced herself.

"Hi," she said warmly. "My name's Estella. I'm new here and looking forward to getting acquainted."

The boys didn't say anything for a long, tense moment.

Then the ginger-haired boy spoke. "Look," he said. "A skunk has got loose in the building."

Estella's eyes narrowed. How dare he call her a name? He didn't even know her. She felt a small ball of rage form as Cruella pushed to be free.

"Ignore them."

Turning, Estella saw a girl about her age standing nearby. She wore the same uniform, but Estella couldn't help noticing the flash of color under the dress shirt. Perhaps there was someone else at this place with a little fashion sense. Estella gave her a grateful smile. "Of course," Estella said, turning her back on the boys. "I'm sure I'll win them over. I'm Estella."

"Anita," the girl answered with a grin.

Just then something wet and hard hit Estella's cheek. Lifting her hand, she found a spitball plastered to the side of her face. She saw the ginger-haired boy and his sidekick laughing. She blinked rapidly, fighting off tears.

Okay, so maybe it was going to take a little longer to win them over.

As the day wore on, it seemed like no matter how hard Estella tried, the other kids were intent on making her first day of school her last. In the hallway there were more spitballs. When she opened her locker, she found it full of garbage. No matter where she went, she heard kids giggling and whispering and even one time caught a student blatantly pointing at her. She had thought her yellow jacket would be her armor. But soon enough, it just made her feel like she stood out–in a bad way.

After lunch, a wholly dreadful experience, Estella sat in the back of a classroom. Her eyes were glued to the clock on the front wall as it slowly ticked by the minutes. All around her she heard snickering. Suddenly, she noticed the boy from earlier–the one with the red hair–sneaking into the classroom. He was late–which wasn't surprising, as Mean Ginger seemed the sort of boy who couldn't be bothered to show up on time to class. And he had an evil look in his eye. That was also not surprising.

He crept up behind the teacher. She was writing notes on the board and didn't notice as the boy carefully pulled her chair back a few inches. It wasn't much, but it was just enough that when the teacher turned to sit, she would likely fall.

It was one thing for the mean boy to pick on Estella, but she couldn't let him humiliate a teacher, too. Estella got to her feet, walked down the space between the desks, and reached for the chair.

Unfortunately, before Estella could move the chair, the teacher turned to sit—and fell flat on her backside. The classroom erupted in laughter.

"This is not how it looks," Estella said, holding up her hands innocently.

From the floor, the teacher glared at her.

"I . . . I . . ." Estella started to protest. But it was no use. The teacher pointed to the door.

Estella walked out, her head high. But as soon as the classroom door shut behind her, Estella let out a trembling breath. Tears welled in her eyes. It was only her first day and she was on the way to the headmaster's office. She was a charity case. A scholarship student. "Your behavior must be impeccable," her mother had reminded her just that morning. Enough blots on her record book and she could lose her place at the school. And now she had just gotten her first blot.

This was supposed to be an amazing day. But now Estella just wanted it to be over.

Chapter 2

Things didn't get better. For the next few weeks, Estella prepared for school like she was readying herself for battle. She didn't want to give anyone the satisfaction of seeing her hurt, so she continued to wear her customized uniform like armor. But inside, she was hurting. Each day brought another round of humiliation. No matter which class she was in or what she said, she was a target. In gym class, dodgeball got her a trip to the headmaster's office for knocking Mean Ginger to the ground—even though he had tried to hurt

Anita first. In art class, Estella's vision for splatter style didn't jibe with the teacher's. Once again, she was off to see the headmaster. Even during school photos, Estella couldn't do the right thing. Her flashy take on the uniform had her pulled out of the photo before the camera bulb went off.

With each demerit, each humiliation, Estella responded with another bright piece of material or a louder dash of paint. They could try, but she wouldn't let them get her down. She wouldn't let them see Cruella. The only place she felt even a bit okay was outside, free from the confines of the stuffy school. But soon enough, even that became a battlefield.

Eating lunch one day, outside and on her own, Estella looked up to see herself surrounded by the mean ginger-haired boy and his equally nasty group of friends. Ginger's cheeks were as red as his hair, and his mean eyes gleamed. Estella hoped perhaps they would just go away.

No such luck.

Ignoring Estella's protests, Mean Ginger and his friends picked her up, carried her to a dumpster, and tossed her in.

Old papers, dirty plates, and old food covered Estella. Digging her way up out of the rubbish, fury on her face, she saw the kids looking down at her. Rage welled up inside her. How dare they? What was their problem? What had she ever done to them? "Why are you so mean?" she shouted as the kids dispersed. But then, out of the corner of her eye, she spotted a glint of something silver and sparkly in the dumpster. Momentarily distracted, she began digging through the trash. Grabbing hold of a bolt of silver fabric, Estella dislodged more trash.

A little whimper sounded.

Estella froze. There was another whimper. Frantically, Estella pawed at the garbage. There was something alive in the dumpster with her! Finally, with a cry, she pulled out a box. Inside was a tiny puppy. It was shivering and whimpering, but as soon as Estella pulled it into her arms, the grateful little creature covered her face in kisses.

At least someone at school seemed to like her.

Estella sat on her threadbare couch at home later that evening, picking at a loose string. Despite the long shower she had taken, she still smelled of garbage. Each whiff sent a fresh new wave of anger flooding through her.

On the floor, the puppy, whom Estella had named

Buddy, sniffed around the furniture, his little tail wagging. *At least you're happy,* Estella thought. *Whoever left you in the dumpster is as mean and nasty as the kids at school.* She had known that starting at a new school was going to be hard. But she had never imagined it would be *this* hard.

Lost in thought, Estella didn't hear her mum come into the room. Her voice startled Estella. "I know that look," her mum said, misinterpreting things. "Thinking up a brilliant design?"

"No," Estella answered. "I was plotting to take them all down."

"Estella . . ." Her mum started to protest.

But Estella shook her head. "I can't just let them do this to me!"

Estella's mum didn't say anything for a moment. She sat down beside Estella and maneuvered their bodies so they were snuggled together. It was comforting, and Estella allowed herself to lean into her mum's warmth. Gently, her mum ran a hand through Estella's hair. First the dark side, then the light. "Turn the other cheek," her mum finally said. "They'll give in. Revenge is not the answer."

Estella sighed. Her mum was right. She always was. Still, the thought of letting those kids get away with treating her badly really rubbed her the wrong way.

With a nod, she stood up and gave her mum a kiss on the top of her head. "I had some great plans for revenge, though," she said. "Really brilliant."

"Save your brilliance for your designs," her mum said.

Estella tried. She really did. But after another few days of being bullied and picked on, Estella decided it was time to use some of her brilliance for revenge after all.

While she found it humorous when Ginger and his buddies opened their lockers and got faces full of green dye, they unfortunately did not.

And, it turned out, neither did the headmaster.

She had a feeling this might have been the last straw.

She was right.

"I think it's clear what's about to happen," the headmaster said after Estella's mum arrived. His hand hovered menacingly over Estella's blot-covered record book. "Estella, you are ex–"

Before he could finish his sentence, Estella's mum got to her feet. "I'm withdrawing her from your school," she stated.

Estella's head swung back and forth between her mum and the headmaster. Her mum's expression was determined. The headmaster's was more stunned–and growing rather angry. He shook his head, his mouth opening and closing. "I'm expelling her," he said, trying to take back control.

"Too late," Estella's mum said, not backing down. "I withdrew her first. So that can't be on the record."

Estella's eyes widened as she realized what her mum had done. If the headmaster had finished his sentence, Estella's record book would be forever marked with an expulsion. She would have a hard time getting into any school with that. Her mum was saving her–again.

"I'd said 'expelled'," the headmaster protested. "I'd already said it."

"Hadn't," Estella said, almost gleeful now that she knew she would never have to come back to the dreaded place or sit in this terrible–not to mention terribly decorated–office ever again.

"Didn't," her mum echoed. She gave her daughter a small smile of reassurance. Turning back to the headmaster, whose face was now a gloriously bright shade of red, her mum added, "And might I say, your school turns out horrible children, with no creativity or compassion."

The headmaster glared at Estella and her mum. "Well, they mostly go work in finance, so we're just doing our job," he explained. Then, as he realized he didn't need to explain himself at all, his face grew even redder and he pointed at the door with a shaking finger. "You're out. Out!"

Estella didn't need to be told twice. She grabbed her record book, shoved it into her bag, and left the office, her mum following.

But once they had walked through the doors and were standing on the other side of the drive, Estella went from triumphant to worried. What had she done? An education had been her one chance at getting out of this town and making a name for herself. Now she was going to be stuck here forever, helping her mum with the sewing. The most excitement she could hope to see would be sewing dresses for her old classmates' formal dances. She tapped her foot in frustration. She had to be "unique". Why couldn't she have just listened to her mum?

Feeling a hand on her shoulder, Estella turned her head. Her mum was staring at her, her eyes watery. That just made Estella feel worse. What were they going to do now?

Chapter 3

Estella was right to be worried. There were consequences. Unfortunately, while Ginger was mean, he was also well-off. He was the youngest son of one of the richest families in town, and as soon as he went running home to tell his parents what had happened, Estella's mum began getting calls. Her services were no longer needed by the well-to-do of the town. By the next day, Estella's mum was without any jobs, Estella was without a school, and they needed a new plan–and a new place to call home.

CHAPTER THREE

There was only one place to go when one needed a fresh start.

London.

After quickly packing their meager belongings into the back of their car, Estella and her mum drove off, leaving their village in the rearview mirror.

Buddy sat on her lap as Estella stared out the window. A part of her felt bad. She was the cause of their sudden departure. But another part of her–a bigger part–was thrilled. London! They were going to London. Home to the hottest designers and most stylish people. They would be sure to appreciate her style there, and she could find a job at a fashion house, and then . . . who knew?!

Estella opened her London guidebook and flipped through the pages. Image after image of huge buildings and bustling streets filled them. She stopped on a picture of a fountain in the center of a beautiful park. Surrounding it were young people dressed in the latest fashion. Everyone was smiling. "London, here we come!" Estella said, unable to contain her excitement.

Her mum looked at her pointedly. "Well, we don't really have a choice," she reminded her daughter. "You have no school. The whole town's turned on you, and I lost a few jobs." She paused. "It's nothing to celebrate."

Estella's excitement dimmed. "I know," she said, lowering her eyes and absently running her fingers across the page of the book. "I'm sorry."

Her mum's expression softened. "You can't be a fashion designer in a small town, anyway," she said.

Lifting her eyes, Estella saw her mum giving her a smile. She smiled back. Maybe this was actually what they had needed all along: a kick in the pants to get them to leave a place that was too confining for Estella's dreams—and hair. Her excitement returning, Estella pointed to the picture of the park. "Can we go here?" she asked.

Estella's mum glanced at the page. "Regent's Park?" she said. While Estella had never left the village, Catherine had spent years in London as a young woman. She nodded, her face brightening. "When we get to the city, first thing we'll do: go to that fountain, have a cup of tea, and start planning how we'll make your dreams come true."

Estella's eyes widened. Was her mum serious? She knew that they had had to leave because they needed to make money, but she hadn't really thought her mother had been thinking about *her* dreams.

CHAPTER THREE

As she stared at her mum, Estella realized something. "Why are you in your best dress?" she asked. She hadn't noticed until then. The dress, with its sharp lines and bright colors, never came out of her mum's closet. In fact, the only time Estella had ever heard her mum yell was when Estella had played dress-up with it.

"I need to make a stop on our way to the city," she answered, "ask a friend for a little help to get us on our feet." Her hands tightened and loosened nervously around the steering wheel as she spoke.

A friend? Estella had never met a single one of her mother's friends. In fact, she didn't know she had any until then. The friend must be someone important, though, given the nice dress and her mother's anxious tone.

"I'll be less trouble from now on," Estella said, trying to ease her mum's worry. "I promise."

Her mother gave her a small smile as the car continued along the road, the gentle rocking creating a calm, lulling effect. Estella leaned her head back. Things were going to be better. She knew it. After everything they had gone through, it was about time she and her mum had a run of good luck.

Estella woke with a start. She had been in the middle of a nightmare where Ginger was as tall as a tower and was chasing after her. Catching her breath, she sat up and looked out the window. Her mum had turned off the main road and they were now making their way down what appeared to be a private lane. A high fence ran along the road.

Suddenly, on the other side of the fence, a huge mansion rose. The house was like something out of a fairy tale. At each corner of the square and imposing building was a round tower. Light poured from the endless windows, and ahead Estella saw a line of cars waiting to drop off people in front of the ornate main door.

A flash of lightning lit up the sky as they turned through a large gate. The road beneath the car's tires turned to gravel, the loud crunching sound jarring Buddy awake. Looking out the window, the little dog growled. Turning to see what was upsetting Buddy, Estella recoiled. There, on the gate, was a large family crest displaying a terrifying three-headed Dalmatian. Lightning flashed again and the name of the estate lit up: Hellman Hall. That made sense.

After bringing the car to a stop, Estella's mum nervously ran her hands over her dress. She shifted the hat on her head and fiddled with the locket she wore around her neck. Estella watched, confused–and curious. She had never seen her mum like this before. Turning, she glanced at the people walking into the fancy estate. Each one looked like they had stepped out of a fashion magazine. *Well, except that one,* Estella thought, noticing a guest wearing what was clearly last year's style. The valet at the door seemed to think the same thing, and he turned the guest away. Apparently, only the fashion-forward would be granted entry. Estella was glad her mother was wearing her fancy dress.

Taking a deep breath, her mum opened the car door and began to get out. Estella moved to follow. Buddy, tail wagging, yipped excitedly.

"You two stay in the car," her mum said resolutely. Once more, her hand went to her neck, and her fingers tugged at the necklace. A look of pain crossed her face, and then she took the necklace off and handed it to Estella.

Estella shook her head. "Wear it," she said. "Looks good."

But her mother insisted. "Looks better without, I think," she said. Then she shrugged. "Be yours one day anyway. Family heirloom. Mind it for me."

Before Estella could protest any further, her mum got out of the car. Once more, Estella tried to follow.

"Estella." Uh-oh. Estella knew that voice. It was her mum's "serious" voice. "Stay in the car. I won't be long."

Through the open door, Estella saw people mingling, crystal glasses in their hands. The air shimmered as sparkling gems and jewels caught the light of what seemed like a thousand candles. Never in her life had Estella wanted to do something more than to go into that party. She looked back at her mum, eyes hopeful. "Mum," she pleaded.

But her mum shook her head. "You might remember a little promise you made earlier?" she said.

Estella sighed. Right. Her promise to be better. Why had she made such a foolish promise?

Her mum gave her a grateful smile. Reaching into the back seat, she grabbed an old gray hat and plopped it onto Estella's head. "I need you to lie low."

"Lay low while wearing a hat?" Estella said, confused.

"Exactly," her mum said. Then, giving Estella and Buddy each a kiss, she shut the door. Pulling back her shoulders, Catherine lifted her head and walked up the front steps.

Estella watched her go, aching to follow. As her mother reached the top of the steps, the valet visibly paled. Estella cocked her head. It seemed like the man recognized her mum. Was he the friend her mum had been talking about?

Before Estella could wonder more, the car shook as thunder rumbled. Another flash of lightning lit the sky, illuminating the huge mansion and making it glow ominously. Beside her, Buddy whined nervously. "Don't worry," she said to the dog. "It'll be okay." She realized she was saying it more to herself than Buddy. There was something in the air that night that made her feel uneasy.

Just then, a woman emerged from a limo, distracting Estella. The woman was wearing the most beautiful gown Estella had ever seen. Pressing her face against the window, Estella took in the lines of the nineteenth-century haute couture gown. "Is that fur and chiffon?" she breathed. "In one gown?"

Her fingers curled around the door handle, itching to open the door. Buddy let out a warning growl. Estella hesitated. She knew she shouldn't do this. But . . . "I just want one teeny, tiny look, Buddy," she said softly, opening the door and stepping fully out of the car. Buddy spilled out behind her. Estella smiled. At least she would have company.

Spotting a servant wheeling a large cart covered in a cloth toward a side door, Estella quickly tiptoed over. While the man's attention was elsewhere, she slipped onto the cart, pulling the cloth over her and Buddy so she was hidden. A moment later the cart shook as it began to move.

She was going inside.

Chapter 4

Estella could barely contain herself. Her fingers twitched, eager to pull back the cloth and peek at all the glorious gowns. But she restrained herself until the cart came to a stop.

Closing her eyes, Estella took a deep breath. Then she opened them, pulling back a corner of the cloth. She suppressed a delighted gasp. It was more incredible than she had imagined. The cart had stopped at the end of a long runway placed in the middle of an enormous ballroom.

Men and women chatted and laughed. They were all dressed in the style of Marie Antoinette's court–high waists, low necklines, wide skirts, and breathtaking colors and patterns. Up on the catwalk, models strutted back and forth in more modern fashions. Estella's heart pounded and her eyes widened with joy. Each model wore something more elaborate and stunning than the last. They were walking pieces of art.

This, thought Estella, nearly crying out with happiness, *is where I belong*.

Just then, another model walked onto the runway. Her long legs took her swiftly down the lane until she stopped, spinning in front of Estella. Close-up, Estella saw that the model's dress had faux squirrels sewn along the bottom, making a furry hem. As the model moved, the squirrels did, too. At her feet, Estella felt Buddy's body stiffen.

He had spotted the squirrels, too.

Before she could stop him, the dog barked and jumped out of the cart.

"Buddy!" Estella cried, scrambling from her hiding spot. "Get back here!"

But the little dog only had eyes for the squirrels. Jumping

up onto the runway, he chased after the model. Estella chased after Buddy. She ducked and weaved, using the huge hoop skirts as camouflage. "This is not laying low," Estella said to herself. As if on cue, a huge spotlight turned on and swept over the runway. For a moment, Estella was illuminated. Her eyes widened, and her breath hitched in her throat. If her mum was somewhere out there, she was totally in trouble.

Luckily, the spotlight swung off her as fast as it had turned on her. Craning her head, Estella watched as it swooped out over the room and toward the enormous stairs that dominated the back wall. There, hovering on a swing above the split stairway, was a woman who made every other woman in the room look pale in comparison.

It wasn't because she was more beautiful–though she was indeed beautiful. It wasn't because she had more jewels on–though she did. And it wasn't because she seemed to magically float in front of a thick swath of drapes. No. It was the way she stood, head lifted, shoulders back. Her entire presence was commanding, full of power, almost like she was a military leader preparing for war. The woman clearly demanded attention–everyone looked at her this way all the time, as they looked at her now.

The woman swung down, the room shocked into silence as she landed at the top of the stairs. With her feet firmly back on the ground, the woman stepped out of the swing. Then, with a grand sweep of her arm, she announced, "Let them eat cake". Behind her, the fabric that Estella thought was drapes then dropped, revealing itself as an elaborate train that attached to the woman's dress. As she moved forward, the train dropped further to reveal a huge cake.

On top, written in bright neon letters that would have made Marie Antoinette's eyes pop, were the same words the woman had just spoken: *Let them eat cake.*

Estella gasped softly. The dress was fashion-forward and absolutely over the top. It was, in a word, brilliant.

As the room erupted in cheers and clapping, Estella's eyes didn't leave the woman. With her chin in the air and her hips swaying, the woman made her way down the stairway step by step. By her side was a trio of huge Dalmatians. The black-and-white dogs had sparkling collars but fierce faces. Estella knew without being told that they weren't the warm and cuddly type. They would protect their owner at any cost.

Finally arriving at the bottom of the stairs, the woman passed the dogs off to a waiting servant and turned to greet her throng of admirers. She held out a hand, turned a cheek, offered thin smiles to the guests. They were like moths to a flame, all drawn to the woman and her unique, commanding light.

The same valet Estella had seen talking to her mother pushed his way through the crowd. Standing on tiptoe, he whispered something into the woman's ear. Her face seemed to flicker with disbelief. Then her eyes darkened. Turning, she stormed out of her own party, disappearing through a door in the back of the ballroom.

His message delivered, the valet turned to go. But as he did, his gaze landed on Estella. His eyes narrowed. Brow furrowed, he began to walk toward her. "You! Come here!"

Shocked–and still a bit dazed by the show the woman had put on–Estella went to run. But she wasn't quite quick enough. The valet's hand closed around her hat, pulling it right off her head. Instantly, her black-and-white hair was on display.

The valet stepped back as though he had been shot. "My god," he breathed. "Put that hat back on before somebody sees . . ."

"What are you, the hair police?" Estella said, pressing the hat back on her head. She began to weave her way out of the ballroom. Then she stopped. Why was she running? Because some stodgy old guy in a penguin suit had an issue with her hair? That was a laugh. Turning, she saw the runway and the cake.

She began to walk toward it. Buddy, no longer distracted by fake fur, joined her. As she got closer to the cake, the details became clearer. Like the dress the hostess wore, no expense had been spared for the luxurious dessert. Estella stopped in front of it. "I was hoping for a piece of cake," she said, a smile tugging on her lips as, out of the corner of her eye, she saw a mixture of fear and anger flash across the valet's face.

"Don't you be cheeky with me," he said, his warning carrying little weight as his expression grew more nervous.

There was no way Estella was getting out of this place through the front door. But maybe . . .

She lifted her hand, then hesitated.

"Don't you dare," the valet threatened. Estella's smile broadened and then, before he could say more, she gave the cake the tiniest of nudges.

That was all it took. Already top-heavy with the ridiculous layers and fondant flowers, the cake immediately began to fall. As guests screamed, Estella ran to the end of the runway and leapt–grabbing hold of the swing the woman had made her entrance on. Below her, the Dalmatians frantically barked, but she stayed safely above them, swinging over them and landing in the middle of a gaggle of guests. Using them as protection, she dashed down a hall. She only hesitated when she heard the clatter of nails on the wood floor. Fearing it was the Dalmatians gaining on her, she sighed in relief when she saw it was only Buddy. She urged him to go faster and continued running. She didn't stop until she raced through an open door and slammed it behind her and Buddy. Her breath coming in gasps, Estella looked up and saw a huge wall of windows. It looked out onto the lawn and the steep cliffs beyond. Lightning flashed and she heard the dogs bark somewhere back near the party. But she didn't care.

She had made it. For now.

Estella's relief did not last long. In the next flash of lightning, she saw two figures standing near the cliff's edge. Moving closer to the window, Estella pressed her nose to the glass, trying to see. Her eyes widened as she realized who the figures were–her mum and a woman she couldn't quite make out.

What is Mum doing out there? Estella wondered.

Behind her, Estella heard the dogs' barking getting louder. At her feet, Buddy whined nervously. She had to get out of there. And while she was at it, she wanted to find out what was going on with her mum. She lifted Buddy into her arms, then pushed open the door and ran out into the dark night.

The wind howled and the sky raged as water lashed at the base of the cliffs below. The Baroness Von Hellman, the evening's hostess and the number one fashion designer in the world, stood at the edge of the cliff, facing Catherine. The woman's surprise arrival at her party had definitely put the Baroness in a mood. She didn't enjoy when her carefully orchestrated plans went awry. And she really despised when those plans were ruined by someone like Catherine. What was the woman even doing here? Their paths had diverged long ago, and the Baroness had made it clear she never wanted to see Catherine again–ever. She had agreed to speak to her only to get her out of the party and away from the other guests. Her reputation could be ruined if the press got wind of mere mortals attending her soirees.

Having led her to the edge of the cliffs, she now waited for the other woman to speak.

"I just need a little help to get us on our feet . . ." Catherine began, tugging nervously at her dress. "My little girl is my life. But I'm afraid that if her spirited streak isn't channeled . . ." Catherine's voice trailed off.

The Baroness heard the pain in Catherine's voice, but her face was a blank mask behind her dramatic makeup. She sighed and looked back at the brightly lit estate as though the entire conversation was nothing more than an inconvenience.

"This is such a dull story." The Baroness's words rang out even over the sound of the waves and the whipping wind. "You have the gall to come back here. And wearing that bland off-the-rack monstrosity."

Catherine once more tugged at her dress, looking back over her shoulder to where the party continued. She seemed to be weighing her next words. "I know things," she said softly. "And the dress isn't that bad."

The Baroness wasn't sure which offended her more: that Catherine would dare imply she could hurt the Baroness, or that she believed the dress wasn't that bad. Both were horribly wrong.

"I just need a little help," Catherine pressed on, unaware of the rage building in the Baroness. "And I'll keep my mouth shut and never come back here."

The Baroness had heard enough. Catherine might have once been her favorite maid, but now she was nothing more than a liability. If she were to leave here and continue to spout nonsense about "knowing" things, it could make the Baroness's life uncomfortable. And the Baroness did not deal with uncomfortable. Staring over at the woman, the Baroness's thoughts grew dark and stormy like the sky above her.

Catherine wanted a little help? Well, the Baroness had

a way of helping them both out. Pulling a whistle from her lips, she blew a silent note into the air.

It was only a matter of moments until this would all be over.

Estella had raced across the lawn and ducked behind a row of perfectly trimmed hedges. Crouching low, she was trying to get a closer look when suddenly she tripped and fell. Gasping, she lifted her head and saw that her mum and the woman had moved even closer to the edge of the cliff.

"Mum!" Estella shouted, no longer caring if she was caught. But her voice was lost amid the roiling sounds of the waves and wind. Estella raced along the hedges. As she got closer, the other woman's voice finally became crystal clear.

"We're done here," she said.

"Mum!" Estella called again from the other side of the hedge. The two women, hearing the noise, turned to look. But Estella was obscured by the tall shrubbery.

Suddenly, a high-pitched ringing sounded in her ears. A moment later she heard the distinct sound of the

Dalmatians' bark. Turning in terror, she saw them racing—right at her!

Ducking down, Estella put her hand on Buddy's back, seeking the comfort of his coat, and closed her eyes. The barks came closer and closer and closer. But at the last moment, instead of attacking her, the dogs leapt over her and the hedge and raced on.

As Estella watched in horror, the dogs' long legs carried them over the grass.

And then, with a final chorus of barks, the dogs were upon her mum.

There was a flash of fabric as her mum lost her footing on the cliff's edge. Her hands flailed in the air. A short scream sounded.

And then there was nothing.

The spot where her mother had just stood was now empty.

Estella couldn't move. She was frozen, staring at where her mum had just been, trying to process what had happened. The dogs, still barking, circled the ground, sniffing wildly as if they might find a trace of her. But they had done their job. She was no more. Her body lay at the bottom of the cliffs.

And Estella was alone.

Still unable to make herself move, Estella heard voices coming from the direction of the house. She only just had time to duck down before the valet appeared, a police sergeant following close behind. A group of guests hovered further back, whispering to each other and pointing.

Suddenly, a large man pushed his way through the crowd. Unlike the guests, he wasn't dressed up, but he was in uniform.

"Police Commissioner Weston." The woman's voice floated over the crowd. "There's been a terrible accident. A woman–she was demanding money. Threatening me. I had no idea the dogs were loose. I think they were . . . chasing someone."

Estella felt a tug on her sweater. But she didn't move. The woman's lies about what Estella's mother had been doing were so clear to her. The tug came again as the commissioner turned to his men and shouted, "Search the grounds!"

The tug came again. More insistent now. Finally, Estella snapped out of her shock. Looking down, she saw that Buddy was whining nervously. She looked up and saw the guards, their flashlights lifted as they began to comb the grounds. The last of her shock faded. Reaching down, she grabbed Buddy and cradled him in her arms.

Then she ran.

Estella didn't stop, even as the sound of the Dalmatians' barking grew louder once more. She raced blindly into the dark, away from the cliff's edge and the horror she had just witnessed. Estella jumped up onto a stone wall as she made her way toward the road. She paused, spotting an open-air truck approaching. She had only a moment to make a decision that would change the course of her life. Stay–and face the woman's wrath. Or jump–and perhaps find safety.

Estella jumped.

She landed with a thud in the back of the open truck. Estella lay there, shivering, surrounded by broken bits of furniture. As the sounds of barking and shouting faded, Buddy popped his head up from inside her jacket and gave her a lick. The gesture, small as it was, broke Estella. She began to sob as her new reality sank in. She was alone. "She's gone, Buddy," she said through her tears. Lifting her hand to her neck, she felt for the necklace her mum had given her.

But like her mum, it was gone, too.

CHAPTER FOUR

Estella woke with a start several hours later. She stretched her stiff limbs and neck, a headache pounding behind her eyes. She must have fallen asleep to the rhythm of the truck's bounce and sway. Sitting up, Estella carefully peeked up over the edge of the truck bed. Her eyes widened

She was no longer in the countryside. Gone were the fences and pastures full of sheep. In their place were huge buildings and dozens of cars parked along narrow streets.

They were in London!

Suddenly, the truck came to a stop as the light in front of it turned red. Estella gasped in recognition. They were right beside Regent's Park–the place she and her mum had planned to go first once they arrived in the city. A fresh wave of grief washed over her, followed by intense longing. Estella knew what she had to do. Grabbing Buddy, she clambered out the back of the truck. As it rumbled away, never the wiser to its temporary occupants, Estella crossed the street and entered the park.

It was beautiful. The moon bathed everything in a magical white glow. Green grass, clipped perfectly, surrounded the round fountain that was composed of three bowl-shaped levels, each one bigger than the one before, all with water cascading from them. As the moonlight caught the falling droplets, they sparkled like diamonds.

The thought of diamonds made Estella think of the woman, and her stomach clenched. Estella walked to the fountain and sat down on a bench. It was damp from the night's dew, but she barely noticed.

"It's all my fault, Buddy," Estella said softly. The words she had thought but dared not say out loud until now tumbled free. "And now . . . she's gone." Exhaustion washed over her. It felt nearly impossible to keep her eyes open. With no strength left to fight, she let them drift closed.

Moments later, Estella was asleep.

Chapter 5

Estella was having the best dream. She stood at the end of a long runway, watching as models wearing her creations sauntered along to incredible bursts of applause. Beside her stood her mum, her face shining with pride. Her mother smiled, turning to her. "I'm so proud of you, Estella," she said. "You've made a name for yourself. Even without me . . ."

Estella blinked awake, the last wisps of her dream disappearing. Sitting up, she saw that morning had come.

Men in suits walked quickly by the fountain, immune

to its beauty. Women, dressed up for the day despite the early hour, walked more leisurely as behind them their nannies pushed their prams.

Suddenly, Estella spotted a boy–around her age, though even worse for wear–crossing to the fountain. A small one-eyed Chihuahua trotted at his heels. The boy's head swiveled left and right and then he pulled out a makeshift fishing rod and began to pull coins out of the fountain with it. Then he dropped them, one by one, into a large sack.

What is he doing? Estella thought. She watched as the boy continued to "fish" for a few more minutes. No one else seemed to notice, and Estella wondered if this was perhaps normal in London.

Her eyes drifted from the fountain and she spotted another boy, as dirty and downtrodden as the other and about the same age as well. With what appeared to be practiced ease, the boy was repeatedly "bumping" into passersby and, under Estella's close gaze, picking their pockets and slipping the stolen wallets or money into his own tattered pants. Estella continued to watch him, transfixed by the casualness and grace with which the boy was executing this petty thievery.

CHAPTER FIVE

Suddenly, sensing someone's eyes on him, the boy looked at Estella.

She gasped and quickly closed her eyes, pretending to be asleep.

The ruse didn't work.

"Morning," said a voice, presumably belonging to the pickpocket.

Estella kept her eyes closed.

"So, what's she?" another voice asked. This one's accent was harsher, his tone less friendly and more reserved.

Estella almost opened her eyes to snap that she wasn't a "what", but thought better of it.

Apparently, the boy hadn't been asking what she was, but rather what she was doing. "Watching us," the first boy answered, "but pretending to be asleep."

"Undercover copper?" the second boy guessed.

"Nah, too scared-looking to be a cop," the other boy said.

"I'm not scared," Estella said, keeping her eyes closed, even though her cover was surely blown. She was beginning to feel slightly foolish. But if she didn't open her eyes, she hoped, maybe they would go away.

No such luck.

"Also looks like twelve years old," the kinder voice observed. "So possibly too young . . ."

Estella had had enough. Snapping open her eyes, she jumped to her feet. To her delight, she startled both boys, who scurried back a few steps. "Stay back!" she commanded, emboldened by their reaction. At her feet, Buddy growled low.

The bigger boy, the one who had been fishing, rolled his eyes. "I'll just take her out." He was the one with the meaner voice. He stepped forward.

But before he could even lift a hand, Estella drew back her leg and kicked him in the gut. He doubled over, cradling his stomach.

"Ow!" he wheezed.

Turning, she looked at the other boy. He was slighter in build and his rosy cheeks gave him a deceptively innocent appearance, but his eyes were tough and streetwise. She stood across from him, fists raised. She wasn't going to let him take her down, either.

"Look, luv," the boy said, keeping his voice calm and level, like he was trying to calm a wild animal. "The cops come by every day at eight a.m. Like clockwork." He paused as if unsure of his next words. Then, in a rush, he said, "You should come with us."

His friend looked up and shot the slighter boy a glare, shaking his head vehemently. "No way," he said. "Just go back to your family, little girl." It was hard to hear him over his wheezing as his face turned a lovely shade of puce.

"She has no family," the thinner, taller boy said when Estella didn't respond.

Her head snapped over to look at him. How did he know? She had barely exchanged a word with him.

"I recognize the look," the boy said, answering her unspoken question.

Tears welled up in Estella's eyes and she angrily brushed them away. He didn't know a thing. Still . . . he was offering her a way to not be alone. It was tempting. Sort of. But before she could speak, Buddy let out a happy little yip. Glancing down, Estella saw that he and the Chihuahua had begun to play. She groaned.

Turning back, she looked at the boy. "I don't even know you," she said softly.

For the first time since they had met, the boy smiled, revealing uneven teeth and a small dimple that Estella might have found charming in a different setting. "I'm Jasper. Pleased to meet you," he said warmly. He pointed at his friend, who still couldn't stand up straight. "That's Horace. Say hello, Horace."

The other boy shook his head. "I'm not saying hello."

Jasper opened his mouth to say something but stopped. Estella followed his gaze across the park to where a cop had appeared. Jasper pulled out a pocket watch. "Five to eight. That's not fair." He pocketed the watch. "We all need to run. Now!"

Estella hesitated only long enough to watch as the cop took out his whistle and blew. She didn't need any more encouragement. Turning, she followed Jasper and Horace as they raced out of the park and onto the streets, with Buddy and the Chihuahua at their heels.

It looked like Estella had just made some new friends.

Jasper ran, every so often checking to be sure the girl was following. He was sure that she had never run that fast or for that long in her life. But to her credit, she kept up. They raced along side streets and over scattered crates, through back gardens of flats; they twisted and turned, making their way out of the ritzy area of London and into its seedier neighborhoods. The cop stayed apace for most of the chase.

Finally, Jasper ducked through a hole in a fence and into the courtyard of an abandoned factory. He kept running toward a hole in the brick siding. Jasper turned. Seeing the girl's hesitation, he gestured for her to follow. She didn't move, her eyes wild, reflecting her inner turmoil. He knew what she was thinking. He had been there before. She was at a turning point. If she moved forward, her world would be forever changed. But if she stayed, the cop was sure to find her, and then what would her life be like? The dog whined at her feet. The noise spurred her forward. It wasn't much of a choice, but it was the only choice she had.

Jasper led them into the brick building and up a flight of stairs to the second storey. The interior staircase was all that was left. The rest of the floor was gone. They kept going, through an open doorway, along a roof, and then Jasper and Horace jumped–disappearing through a coal chute in a ceiling. Behind them, the girl took a deep breath and did the same.

Jasper landed with a thud on a pile of mattresses and

got to his feet. Beside him, Horace was mumbling something to himself about a secret hideout and not showing her. But it was too late. She had already seen it.

"Where are we?" the girl asked, standing up. Her clothes were covered in a fine layer of black soot.

"Home sweet home," Jasper answered.

The girl gazed around the space, her expression skeptical. Jasper's own gaze followed as he tried to see the space through her eyes. There were a few more mattresses on the floor and what must have once been a rug but now looked more like a rag. A chair with only three working legs wobbled precariously in a corner, and the only light came through a large stained glass window at the end of the room.

Home? Maybe. Sweet? That was questionable.

Ignoring her skeptical look, Jasper took a seat on one of the cleaner mattresses. "So, what's your story?" he asked. She was in their lair; they might as well become friendly.

Horace, however, did not seem obliged by social custom. "Where are your parents?" he asked sharply.

Immediately, the girl's eyes welled with tears. Jasper shifted uncomfortably. He and Horace shared helpless glances, not knowing what to do other than wait silently as the girl's tears dried and she pulled herself together.

"My mum's dead," she finally said, answering both their questions, her strong tone a contrast to her tear-streaked face.

Jasper nodded. He had expected that answer. "I'm thinking," he said after a moment, "you should stay here. Be part of our gang . . . ?" He trailed off, hoping she would take the bait and tell them her name.

"Estella," she answered.

Jasper smiled. But Horace now wore the same pained expression as when Estella had gut-kicked him. "She should what?" he said in exasperation. He shook his head. "This has not been discussed."

"We could use a girl to be a distraction, help us look innocent," Jasper pointed out.

Horace cocked his head. "She does look really sad and scrawny and pathetic and helpless—" He didn't get further, as Estella walked over and punched him in the arm. "Oy! Why do you keep hitting me?"

"It only happens when you talk," Estella replied, earning her a grin from Jasper and another frown from Horace.

She paused. "You're criminals," she said, the word sounding harsher when she spoke it aloud.

Jasper shrugged. "You say 'criminals'. I say 'entrepreneurs'."

"I want to be a fashion designer, not a thief," she said softly.

"That's funny," Horace said. "You're a little kid."

Estella opened her mouth to protest. But Jasper interrupted. "He's right," he said. "You don't got that many options, Estella. Just us."

Estella sank down on a nearby mattress. Jasper's frank words seemed to take the fight out of her. She put her head in her hands.

"Is she crying again?" Horace whispered loudly.

"Her mum died," Jasper said. "You remember what that's like."

Horace was silent for a moment. "Yeah, I do," he finally said, his tone a bit softer than before.

At his words, Estella looked up. As she did, her hat tumbled from her head, revealing her hair. Horace yelped. Self-consciously, the girl brushed it back and reached for her hat. "It has to go," she said.

But Jasper stopped her. "I quite like it," he said simply, earning him a small smile.

Still, she was right. Hair like that was too recognizable. If she was going to become one of them, she would need to be able to blend in, hide, be unremarkable. Horace seemed to have the same thought. He stood up, walked to a box on the ground, and began to rummage around. A moment later he straightened up, a bottle in each hand. "Red or yellow?" he asked.

Leaving her hat on the floor, Estella stood up and made her way to the Lair's lone bathroom. She shut the door behind her, and for a while, the only sound to be heard was that of running water.

When Estella finally emerged, the black-and-white hair was gone. She was now a redhead. She tilted her head from side to side.

Not bad, Jasper thought.

"So," she said, ignoring their curious looks, "how's it work?"

Jasper smiled. "Don't worry," he said. "We'll start you off with the simple stuff."

It was time to teach Estella how to be a thief.

Jasper was true to his word–which Estella found somewhat ironic, given he was a thief. But like he promised, he started her off with the "simple stuff".

First there was the basic Adam Tyler, as Jasper called it. It was a quick pickpocketing move; the most difficult part was getting everyone–dogs included–to work together. While Horace bumped into a passerby, Estella would pick their pocket and drop it into Buddy's open mouth. A quick trot over to Jasper ended with sleight of hand. Before the target even turned the corner, the wallet was on the ground, empty, and the gang was heading the other way–pockets full. Simple.

But the moves got harder. Fast.

And Estella learned them all–faster.

She learned how to pickpocket. She learned how to be the distraction. She learned how to spot an undercover cop and how to scope a mark. She mastered the Waterworks–a move that involved making a driver mistakenly think they had hit Buddy and always ended in tears–and even managed to make up a few moves of her own.

CHAPTER FIVE

To Estella's surprise, she quickly adapted to her new life. When they weren't out on the streets being "entrepreneurs", Estella threw herself into making her new home feel a bit more . . . well, homey. She replaced the dirty mattresses with newer ones. Rummaging through the garbage cans in the fancy parts of town, she found barely used art and pillows, plates and decorations. With Jasper's help, she dragged them back to the Lair, and before long the walls were no longer bare. A few lights brightened the space, and Estella even managed to find room dividers so she could have a space of her own.

The Lair taken care of, Estella turned her attention to the boys. While they were pulling in decent money with their regular heists, she knew they could do more. The only problem was they were limited in where they could go. They had minimal clothing, and even fewer ways to really clean that clothing. More often than not their clothes were stained, ripped, or patched. If they wanted to steal from the rich, they were going to need to look, well, richer–or at least look more like the people who worked for the rich.

With a new goal set, Estella quickly formulated a plan. She had the talent to make them all look better. The rest would fall into place. She just needed to get her hands on one special item . . .

A few nights later, she and the boys were standing at the back entrance of a tailor's shop. They shifted uncomfortably on their feet. The street was too quiet. They were too obvious. This wasn't their typical mark and they didn't like it.

But as Estella had pointed out earlier, they needed to get inside and get what Estella was after. "We could be bigger, better . . . richer," she had told them. "You just have to trust me. I know what I'm doing."

She had gotten Horace at "richer". Jasper was still uncertain. But she did know what she was doing. Standing on her tiptoes, she propped open a little window above the door. Horace squeezed their Chihuahua–Wink–through the window, and they heard him land lightly on the other side. A moment later there was a scrabbling at the back door and it swung open. Tiptoeing inside while the boys kept watch, Estella made her way over to the tailor's workbench. There, gleaming even in the dim light, was a brand-new sewing machine.

Estella's heart filled at the sight of it. She hefted it into her arms, taking a deep, satisfied breath. Then, turning, she fled the shop. The boys followed close behind.

From that moment on, it was Estella who came up with their "jobs". She sewed altar boy costumes for Sundays so Horace and Jasper could collect for the "needy". She created butler uniforms and sent them out to serve the rich and famous and help themselves to their pockets. She whipped up costume after costume with stolen fabric and a wild imagination, while the boys watched in awe.

Estella was happy. She didn't realize it at first, but while she still thought of her mother every time she opened her eyes or walked by a fountain or saw a flash of bright fabric, the pain had become just a dull ache. She had a new life now. While it wasn't one she could ever have imagined when she lived in her cottage, it wasn't all that bad. She could sew; she had friends; she had a roof over her head (even if it leaked). Yes, she was happy.

And in this state of general contentment, the years passed by.

Chapter 6

THIRTEEN YEARS LATER

Squinting, with her tongue poked out in concentration, Estella sat at her sewing machine. The steady sound of the machine soothed her and drowned out the other noises of the Lair: the sound of Horace's shouting at the television, the dogs' incessant yapping, Jasper's loud footsteps as he stomped around the floor below. Occasionally she would sit up and stretch, her shoulders tight from another long night of sewing. When she did, she couldn't help smiling.

CHAPTER SIX

Over the years, her part of the Lair had come to look every bit like a fashion designer's work space. Racks of clothes, from gaudy cop uniforms to elaborate formal attire, lined the space, creating three walls of costumes surrounding her. Pictures of models in various modes of dress were tacked on the actual walls and scattered about the floor. Sketches of outfit ideas–some complete, others in the early stages–were piled on a table. A few mannequins stood at precarious-seeming angles, wearing bits and pieces of clothing.

Estella turned back to the machine. Her foot pressed down on the pedal and the needle pumped up and down. She knew she didn't have much time before Horace and Jasper interrupted, and she was desperate to finish this one piece.

"Estella!"

Jasper's voice startled Estella, and her foot slipped off the pedal. Turning, she saw him standing at the far end of the Lair. In the years that had passed he had grown taller, but no wider. He was a beanpole, with a shock of brown hair that never seemed to stay in place unless stuffed under a hat. But his eyes were the same–gentle, kind, and wise.

Only at the moment, there was a bit of impatience in them.

"We're on!" Jasper said.

Estella jumped to her feet and brushed past the racks of clothes, grabbing three costumes on the way. In the center of the Lair, Horace was sitting on the couch, watching a soccer match on one of their more recent acquisitions–a television. He was wearing a jersey of the team and his face was as animated as it ever got. The jersey strained against his middle as he cheered.

Spotting Estella and Jasper, he shook his head. "Two minutes? Please?" he begged. "It's stoppage time."

Jasper shook his head. "Now," he said.

Estella suppressed a smile as Horace groaned and pushed himself to his feet. It still amused her to see the boys banter, even after all these years. They were like an old married couple. Although, she thought now, did that make her their sister? Or daughter? She shook her head. She didn't like either. No, she was their partner–in crime, at least.

She threw the evening's outfits at Jasper and Horace, and they all quickly made their way out of the Lair. It was time to go to work.

CHAPTER SIX

On the way to their mark–a fancy restaurant in the theater district–Jasper and Estella got ready. Arriving in front of the restaurant, they were dressed immaculately. Estella wore a gown, Jasper a suit. They slipped inside and waited by the coat check for a few moments–just long enough to empty the pockets of a few diners before stepping back outside, where Horace was pulling up in an expensive car. He jumped out, and Estella nodded satisfactorily at her handiwork. His valet costume was spot-on. As they slipped into "their" car, Horace flipped his jacket inside out, revealing a regular dinner coat underneath. The real valet was none the wiser as Horace gave him a nod and walked down the street.

Job one was a wrap.

But in their line of work, there was always another job. The next day found them in the Financial District, with Estella, dolled up in a tight dress and sky-high heels, sashaying through crowds of rich businessmen. As the men helped themselves to an ogling eyeful of Estella's long legs, her friends helped themselves to the men's wallets. Later that afternoon, in a jewelry shop, Estella perused the counters, a gloved finger to her lip as she acted every inch the rich debutante. "I must have something sparkling," she said over her shoulder to Jasper, her voice as posh as the dress she had sewn. And just like that, a set of diamond earrings and a matching necklace appeared–only to disappear a moment later when Buddy barreled into the store and provided a perfect distraction.

And so it went, day after day, and job after job. Estella's outfits got them in, and their cunning got them rich–or rich enough. It never seemed like they could hold on to their earnings. So the Lair remained home. Estella didn't mind. Her shares of the profit always went to buying more fabric, more material for costumes and her dream designs. She just wished there were something more in store for them.

Maybe, even, more for her?

Estella stared out a floor-to-ceiling window. She and the boys were in the middle of some "housekeeping". Only in this case, the house was a hotel room and the cleaning was more like a complete wiping out. Estella absently picked up objects, but her eyes never left the window. Across the street was a giant billboard advertising the latest Baroness designs. A line of gowns spread across the house-sized sign, each one bolder and brighter than the one before.

"What's wrong?"

Jasper's voice startled her. Begrudgingly, she turned her gaze from the dresses and saw Jasper standing in the doorway. Estella recognized the peculiar look on his face. It meant he was curious–or confused–about something. She shrugged and walked past him into the hall, handing him a wallet as she went.

"Just bored," she said.

"Bored?" Horace had popped out of the room he had been "cleaning" and joined the pair. "Are you kidding? I found a tiny TV. And a guy asleep on the bed. Look." He nodded over his shoulder. Estella peered into the room. Sure enough, there was a man sound asleep. She laughed. Leave it to Horace to clean *around* someone.

Suddenly, the stairwell door opened at the end of the hall. All three turned and watched as the hotel manager appeared. He spotted them instantly. "Who are you three?" he said loudly.

"Run," Jasper whispered out of the corner of his mouth. It was their usual getaway plan.

But Estella was bored of running, just like she was bored of doing the same stints day in and day out. She wanted a change. She needed to do something to make it feel like she wasn't falling into a rut.

It was time for a bit of fun.

Shaking her head at Jasper, she turned and strode toward the manager. Behind her she heard Jasper try to call her back. She ignored him.

"Who are we?" she asked, taking on a cockney accent. "I'll tell you who 'we' are. We are from Hotel Consultants Group, and we've been undercover, reporting for the head honchos of this greasy palace on the standards we have found."

The manager's mouth dropped open. He stood there, stammering, as Estella rolled on.

"And one word has come to mind." She looked down her nose at the manager. "Sloppy."

"Sloppy," Jasper echoed, joining in. "A damning report is in the works."

"However, lucky for you, Frederick," Estella went on, reading the name tag on the manager's jacket, "assistant manager, we can single you out as the shining star in the sloppy darkness."

Finally finding his voice, Frederick nodded. "Thanks, I–"

"For a price, of course," Estella said, cutting him off. She held out a hand.

As the manager reached for his wallet, Estella gave Jasper a wink. She was bored, maybe, but that didn't mean she didn't love her job.

Later that night, Estella lay on her bed, staring up at the fashion shots she had taped to the ceiling. Images of the Baroness's billboard from earlier floated in front of her. It had been fun to do something different back at the hotel, but after the high had faded, she was back to feeling restless. She had been pulling heists for so long now. And with every job, she felt a bit of her childhood dream fade. What would her mum think if she could see her now? Lying in the Lair, with nothing to claim as her own except dozens of costumes used to rob people of their possessions, Estella grimaced. She doubted it would be anything good.

Hearing footsteps, Estella turned as Jasper and Horace entered her room. A smile replaced her sad frown as she saw that they were carrying a large cake ablaze with over two dozen candles. Buddy and Wink trotted at their feet, each one wearing a party hat.

Her birthday. She had completely forgotten.

Beaming, she stood up. "This is the nicest birthday since . . ." she said after she blew out the candles, "my mum was around." Her eyes started to well with tears, and she brushed them away. She didn't want to cry. Not that night.

Jasper nodded. But instead of saying anything, he simply handed her an envelope.

"What's this?" she asked, confused.

"This," Jasper said as a smile began to spread across his face, "is an offer of employment at Liberty of London."

Horace cocked his head. Clearly, he hadn't been in on the gift. "Is it a hamburger place? Because that would be great."

Estella couldn't believe it. It wasn't a hamburger place. It wasn't even close. Liberty of London was the most fashionable department store in the city. "How did you . . ." She trailed off, shocked.

Jasper shrugged. It hadn't taken much, he told her. Just some basic sleight of hand and a bit of distraction to drop an application–filled out by him, with Estella's photo attached–onto the "accepted" tray. Well, maybe it had taken a bit of effort, Jasper added when Estella expressed disbelief. There might have been a close call as he dangled from a skylight over the secretary's desk. But nothing some quick maneuvering couldn't fix.

A thousand emotions flooded Estella. Joy. Fear. Surprise. Admiration. Jasper had just given her the greatest gift any person could give her. A chance to work in a department store filled with all the latest fashions? To be surrounded every day by all that fabric, all that beauty? It was a dream come true.

"I love Liberty!" she shouted, letting the excitement bubble over and out.

Jasper grinned sheepishly. "I know," he said. "I've seen how you look at it as we pass. Now, I might have padded your CV a bit," he added. "As in completely. Invented a few references. If anyone asks how you know Prince Charles, just say it's a polo thing."

Looking back and forth from the paper in her hand to Jasper, Estella beamed. Then she reached out and threw her arms around Jasper. "Thank you!" she said, hugging him hard.

Horace looked confused. "So what's the angle?" he asked. It wasn't an odd question. They usually had an angle. Was this going to be a way to do an inside job? Scope out a new mark?

But Jasper shook his head. "There's no angle."

"Right," Horace said. "But really. What is it?"

"The angle is Estella should get a shot at being big out there because she's too talented to be doing grifts with the likes of me and you," Jasper said. His words surprised Horace into silence. Turning, he smiled at Estella.

Warmth filled her and she felt her cheeks flush. Shaking her head, she thanked him again. And then she punched him in the arm, because that's what Estella tended to fall back on when the right words eluded her. And also because they were friends and that was what friends did.

They also, it seemed, helped make dreams come true.

Chapter 7

Estella stood in front of the Liberty department store. Her hands nervously tugged at the bottom of her shirt as she stared up at the imposing Tudor facade. On either side of her, people brushed past, entering through the spinning doors and disappearing inside. For so long she had only dreamed of being a part of a place as spectacular as Liberty. And now it was about to become a reality.

Before arriving for her first day, Estella had stopped by

Regent's Park. Over the years she had made a tradition of going there with two cups of tea and saying "hello" to her mum. She'd fill Catherine in on a spectacularly good heist or show her a sketch of a dress design she was particularly fond of. It helped Estella feel close to her mum–even though she was gone.

That day, she had sat on a bench in front of the fountain, a second cup of tea by her side. As she took a small sip, she said, "Mum, I got my chance. The one I've always wanted." She smiled and lifted a hand to her red hair as she imagined her mother's nose crinkling as she reminded her to be a kind girl. "I'm going to keep my head down and make it," she added. Then, with one quick "cheers", she had put her teacups in her bag, stood up, and made her way to Liberty. Now all she had to do was walk through the doors.

But her feet felt frozen. This was scarier than any heist with the gang. Because this meant so much more.

Taking a deep breath, she smoothed her hands over her shirt and walked inside.

She gasped. She couldn't help it. She had been there a handful of times over the years–just to wander the aisles and pretend for a moment that this could be her life–and yet each visit to the store literally took her breath away. Its ceilings rose high into the air, melding Gothic style with modern metal and glittering glass. Carved wooden balconies encircled a huge multi-storey atrium that was filled with every type of department imaginable. Slowly, Estella moved through the cosmetics section, past the jewelry counter, and by the racks of haute couture. Nearby, a group of eager young women were standing at the ready to help shoppers fulfil their every need. She scanned the area, looking for someone who might be able to help her. But all she saw were shoppers dressed to the nines, their arms full of bags. The richer patrons didn't even bother carrying their own goods. They had men dressed in Liberty uniforms following them, pushing carts or carrying arms full of clothes.

"Estella?"

At her name, Estella turned. A man, face pinched tight and a clipboard in hand, was staring at her. His foot tapped impatiently. This, Estella deduced, was her boss. She quickly walked over and fell into step behind him as he led her deeper into the bowels of the store. As he walked, he talked. Her job, he informed her, was not to dawdle among the departments. It was not to help with alterations or offer her advice on window design. Her job, he said, with far too much satisfaction, was to clean up after the patrons.

Estella tried not to let her face show her surprise. She had just assumed she would be working in the fashion department.

But she was wrong. Terribly wrong.

Estella was working in the janitorial department.

Shoving open the door to the employee bathroom, Estella pushed a bucket full of dirty water in front of her, frowning as she caught sight of her reflection in the mirror. The janitorial uniform was drab and, she was rather sure, had not been washed in a decade. Her hair was falling out of its neat bun and there were smudges of dirt on her cheeks. She glanced down at her hands. The lacquer she had put on that first day she had walked into Liberty had long since been chipped away.

She grimaced. This was not her dream job. This was a nightmare.

Every day since she had started, she had tried to sow the seeds for a swift exit from janitorial and into the fashion department. She had greeted salesgirls with smiles, offered up thoughts to the seamstresses sewing in the basement, even tried to ingratiate herself with the perfume girls who only had to stand and spritz fragrance. But no matter what she did or who she talked to, she was met with the same cold, condescending stares. It was clear where Estella stood–the very bottom.

Just then her boss, Gerald, whom she was pretty sure just stood about waiting to see if he could catch her messing up, walked by. He glanced at her, and then looked down at his clipboard and checked something off. *Just like the headmaster at school,* Estella thought. *Marking me down in his record book.*

"Please, sir," she said, greeting Gerald as warmly as she could. Carefully putting down the garbage bags she had been taking to the dumpster, she approached him. "Sir," she went on. "I'm a dab hand with a needle, perhaps alterations could use–"

"Why are you talking and not cleaning?" Gerald answered.

Estella sighed as he walked away. "You wouldn't regret it . . ." she finished hopefully. But the man was too far away to hear.

Turning, Estella picked up the bags and continued to the back alley. Hauling the garbage to the large dumpster, she struggled to lift the first one. It missed the dumpster completely and landed on the far side. Estella groaned. As if the day couldn't get any worse.

"So it's glamourous, isn't it?"

Turning, she saw Jasper and Horace standing in the alley, looking at her with amused expressions.

"You forgot your lunch," Jasper added, holding up a brown bag. "How's it going?"

Estella straightened her shoulders. She could answer honestly–the day had been awful so far and she wanted to give up. Or she could do what her mum had always taught her–focus on the brighter side of things. She went with option two.

"It's a world of opportunity, just like you said. I will rise, trust me," she said, hoping to convince herself as much as them. "I am calm and patient."

Both boys laughed. Those were not words typically associated with Estella.

"I know you will," Jasper said, straightening his smile and giving her a nod.

Estella shot him a grateful look, and as she did, she noticed Horace eyeing an open window above the dumpster. She shook her head. "No."

"No what?" Horace said, trying–and failing–to act innocent.

"No, I'm not letting you in that window so you can try and crack the safe," Estella said.

Horace shook his head. "That's not the angle?"

"There's no angle!" Estella and Jasper shouted together.

Laughing, Jasper tugged on Horace's sleeve, leading him away from Estella. At the end of the alley, he turned and lifted a hand to Estella. She raised one back.

Sighing, Estella turned back to her task at hand and picked up the next trash bag, heaving it up toward the dumpster. This one hit the mark, but it also managed to hit a loose piece of metal sticking up. There was a ripping sound, and the bag opened, pouring orange peels, old coffee grounds, and other remnants all over her.

"Really?" she shouted to no one in particular. Tossing the remaining bags into the dumpster, Estella turned to go back inside, covered in garbage. She needed to change.

Now. But when she went to turn the handle, it wouldn't move.

She was locked out.

Estella groaned loudly. Finding the bright side was going to be hard.

She turned from the door and walked down the alley and to the front of Liberty. A few passersby gave her curious looks, and she hunched her shoulders, as if that could obscure the janitorial uniform and bits of trash sticking to her. Just as she reached the main doors, she spotted movement in one of the display windows. She lifted her eyes.

A woman, not much older than her, was tentatively moving a mannequin's arm and then rearranging a scarf so that it draped lower on the left than the right. Estella shook her head. The window was awful. The clothing the woman had chosen was drab and uninspired. Even the furniture the stylist had chosen to "create the space", was dull. Nothing went together. There was no theme. No message. It was as though the stylists had closed their eyes and grabbed a handful of items and just thrown them on the mannequins.

Before she knew what she was doing, Estella found herself tapping on the window. The woman looked up and cocked her head, confused. "I feel sad that you think that looks good," Estella said.

What? the woman in the display window mouthed.

"I feel sad that—" Estella stopped yelling as her boss walked into the display. She froze. His eyes met hers and narrowed. Crooking his finger, he gestured for her to get inside. She didn't need to hear him to know he meant *now*.

Giving the terrible window one last pitying glance, Estella made her way back into the department store. Instead of keeping her head down and skirting along the side to the back area, like she was sure her boss wanted, Estella took a deep breath, raised her head high, and sauntered right through the middle of the place. She was more than likely about to lose her job. So why not go out being true to who she was–and that was someone who knew fashion and didn't need this job.

As she passed smartly dressed women, she nodded. "Afternoon," she said to one. "Lovely scarf," she said to another older patron, who was holding up two scarves underneath her wrinkled chins, trying to choose. "Whatever covers your neck more." This was met with a look of shock from the patron but made Estella smile.

Finally, she reached her boss. She stopped and waited for the inevitable dressing-down.

"You have a circular slice of banana on your cheek," Gerald pointed out coldly.

Estella removed the banana. Then, as her boss watched, she popped it into her mouth. She tried not to laugh outright at his look of disgust. She hadn't survived on the streets for as long as she had without growing a backbone that was clearly stronger than his.

As if sensing something had changed in Estella, Gerald signaled for her to follow him to the office. "Finish out the day," he said when they arrived and he had shut the door behind them. Walking toward his desk, he gave Estella a stern look as he said, "Clean my office from top to bottom. Then give your uniform back and get a bus back to whatever tiny pathetic life you come from."

Estella's head snapped up in her surprise. "That seemed uncalled for," she said. Figuring she had nothing left to lose, she added, "I think under that starchy half-size-too-small bum-clencher of a suit might lurk a kind man who would like to give a brilliant kid another shot."

Apparently, however, there was no kind man lurking anywhere. "Clean! Now!"

A little while later, Estella surveyed Gerald's immaculate office. Outside, it was getting dark. Suddenly, Horace's words came back to her. "What's the angle?" Well, there hadn't been one. Not before. But maybe she had been too fast to brush that idea off. Maybe there was an angle she could work after all.

Estella sighed with pleasure as she removed her smock and let her hair down from its elastic. It felt good to loosen up for a moment.

Now on to the real job.

By the time she left the office, the moon was out, and the store was empty. Estella made her way to the front of the store, jumping at its sounds as it settled into its after-hours emptiness. Spotting the door to the display window, she shouted. The sad, sad window! She could fix it.

Stepping into the storefront, she tiptoed over to the

mannequin that had caught her eye earlier that day. Even in the dark, the outfit was atrocious. "I just can't leave you looking like that," she said to the inanimate figure. "It would be cruel."

Tearing off the mannequin's hat, Estella got to work.

Estella was having a terrible nightmare. She was in a dumpster and someone kept hitting the sides of the large metal container. Bang. Bang. Bang. Over and over again. Why wouldn't they stop? In her nightmare, the banging grew louder and more insistent. Estella opened her mouth to scream—and then she woke up.

Opening her eyes, Estella gasped. The banging hadn't been a nightmare. It had been Jasper and Horace! They were standing outside the window display staring at her.

And they were accompanied by a crowd of onlookers growing by the moment.

Oh no, oh no, oh no! Estella thought as she clambered to her feet. She must have fallen asleep after she'd finished playing with the window display. She turned and looked at the display. Despite the fear coursing through her, she couldn't help smiling. The window was brilliant. She had found a can of spray paint and graffitied the back wall. One of the mannequins' stodgy dresses had been replaced with a leather jacket paired with proper trousers, while the other was dressed in neon. She had even managed to bring life to the furniture, adding pops of texture and color that clashed and yet went together. It was a whole new window–bright, bold, messy, and provocative.

Estella bit her lip as she studied her work. Bright, bold, messy, and provocative was not exactly Liberty. But it was so her.

She couldn't help smiling proudly. Turning to the mannequins, she winked. "Seriously. How much better is that? You both look happier."

Hearing a rap at the window, she held up a hand. Jasper and Horace could wait. "I'll be out in a–" The rapping continued. Estella looked over her shoulder and gulped. It wasn't Jasper. Or Horace. It was Gerald.

"Oh dear," she said. The man looked incensed. Sighing, Estella let herself out of the window display just as the front doors of Liberty opened for business. As crowds of people streamed in, she saw her boss making a beeline for her.

"You!" he shouted. "Stay there! I'm calling the police!"

Police? That seemed a bit much. She hadn't done anything—except fix a fashion crime. Really, the stylist was the one who should be arrested. But apparently her boss didn't see it the same way. He kept shouting for the police. Estella turned. The security guards at the front door had spotted her and were moving toward her. And there were more emerging from the back of the store. She had nowhere to run.

Spotting Horace, she saw that he had made his way inside and was now too busy picking her boss's pocket to help. And she couldn't see Jasper through the early morning rush of shoppers. Frantically she tried to think of a plan. But escapes had always been Jasper's thing. Not hers. She was fresh out of ideas.

Suddenly, one of her boss's minions ran up to him. He was shaking and his breath was coming in gasps. "She's coming! The Baroness!"

At his words, her boss went pale. Spinning around, he clapped his hands together, the sound echoing through the store and making every employee—and a few customers—stop in their tracks. "Battle stations, everyone!" Gerald ordered.

Estella wasn't about to miss an opportunity to jet. Turning, she ran, ducking down and hiding behind one of the overstuffed display cases.

Suddenly, out of the corner of her eye, she finally spotted Jasper. He crawled over and crouched down next to her. "Is there a back way out?" he whispered.

Estella shook her head. She didn't want a way out. Not yet, at least. Not until she saw–her. "Did you hear that?" she asked, almost forgetting to keep her voice down. "The Baroness. I want to see her."

Jasper looked at her like she had gone mad. "They're distracted!" he hissed. "Let's go."

But Estella ignored him, her eyes trained on the front door. A moment later, a large bodyguard and two smaller security guards entered.

The Baroness followed.

Estella's breath hitched as she took in the fashion designer. She looked just like the images that plastered the front page of any society magazine or paper. Estella couldn't stop staring. The woman practically dripped condescension. Her mouth was pulled down in disdain and her eyes were ice. But Estella barely registered that. All she saw was how impossibly chic the woman looked in her designer outfit.

"That's her," she said.

Jasper rolled his eyes. He opened his mouth to speak, but was stopped by the sound of the Baroness's voice cutting across the atrium. "Outside," she snapped. "That window display."

Nervously, the boss stepped forward. "I'm so sorry," he said, his voice shaking. "I can explain . . ."

Feeling a tug on her sleeve, Estella dragged her eyes from the pair. Jasper was frantically nodding toward the end of the display case. The security guards had spotted them. "You're right," she said. "Time to go!"

Chapter 8

Estella tried to get to her feet. Beside her, Jasper did the same. But they weren't quick enough. Jasper went down first as a security guard grabbed him and tackled him. Another security guard stepped in front of Estella before she made it past the display case. The guard put his hand atop Estella's head and shoved it down so her cheek was pressed against the cold display case. Estella struggled, but there was no getting away from his grip.

"Sorry, Baroness," Gerald said. "This is the vandal who messed up the whole window display. We'll deal with it."

There was a moment of silence. Estella wished she could see the Baroness's face, but all she could see were the gems in the case below. Finally, the woman spoke. "She works here?"

"She was fired," Gerald said quickly. "We try to give these wretches a chance but . . . breeding . . ." Estella mumbled something, prompting the security guard to smoosh her face harder against the unforgiving glass of the display case.

"So she doesn't work here?" the Baroness clarified.

"I . . . I . . ." he stuttered. He clearly wasn't sure what the Baroness wanted him to say.

The Baroness shook her head. "You're sweating," she said. The comment made Estella smile despite her situation. "And I can smell you. Step back."

"Agreed. Brilliant," he said quickly, causing Estella's smile to broaden. It was fun to see her boss be the one in the hot seat for once.

"You, grubby girl." The Baroness's voice had shifted. Craning her head to the side as best she could, Estella saw the Baroness was looking at her. The older woman gestured to a slight man who had been standing off to the side. "Jeffrey," she said, "card."

With a nod, Jeffrey hustled toward Estella. He reached into the front pocket of his suit and pulled out a card. "You're hired," he said. "This address. Five a.m. Don't be late." He tried to hand her the card, but the security guard wouldn't let her go.

"Teeth," Estella said, for that was the only way she could possibly grab the card.

Gingerly, Jeffrey placed the card in front of Estella's mouth. She quickly snatched it and then, shrugging off the guard's grasp, freed herself. At the same time, Jasper slid free of his captor. As if on cue, Horace reappeared, with bags of stolen loot dangling from both hands.

Not waiting to see how the rest of the moment would play out, the three bolted. Behind them, the Baroness observed this all with a sort of detached curiosity. Just as Estella reached the door, she heard her say to Gerald, "You're a fool. That girl has put together the best window display that I've seen you do in ten years."

As the trio slid out of the store and onto the busy sidewalk, Estella couldn't stop smiling. The card was clenched in her hand. It was real. The Baroness had liked her window! And even better, she had a new job. A job with the Baroness. Forget Liberty. She was moving on up.

They hopped into the back of an open truck and headed home to the Lair. Estella couldn't stop staring at the card. It was beautiful, creamy and thick. It looked important–just like the woman who had given it to her. Written across the middle, in bold cursive, were the words *Baroness Enterprises*; beneath that was an address in a smaller font. Estella ran her hand over the lettering, the raised letters making her shiver.

When the truck lumbered by the Lair, she and the boys jumped out. Still, Estella didn't look up from the card. Once safely inside, Estella plopped down on her bed and held up the card. "She liked my window, Jasper." Her voice was soft as she met Jasper's gaze. He had been patiently waiting for her to talk. "She liked my window!"

Jasper smiled. "I'm happy for you," he said.

She returned the smile. "All thanks to you."

Horace, who had been busily sorting through the loot from the store, looked up. "Is this the angle?" he asked.

Estella laughed. He was incorrigible. But she didn't care. There was no angle. Starting tomorrow morning, she was finally going to take the fashion world by storm.

CHAPTER EIGHT

Five a.m. came quickly. Estella had spent most of a restless night too excited to sleep, and when she did sleep, her dreams were filled with heads of mannequins and bolts of fabric. By the time her alarm went off, she had already been dressed and ready to go for an hour.

Now she stood in front of a huge warehouse. The sun hadn't yet risen, so the street was dark save for the occasional lamp that flickered. The large doors had not yet opened, and Estella shifted nervously on her feet. She looked down at the card, clutched in her hand, to check the address once again.

Suddenly, the door burst open. Jeffrey, the Baroness's assistant, looked out at her. "Ah, you," he said as though surprised to see her, even though he had been the one to tell her where to be and when. "Come in."

Estella didn't hesitate. As Jeffrey led her into the warehouse, Estella's head swiveled back and forth; she was desperate to take it all in. From the outside, the warehouse had looked like any other. But inside it was completely different. Soft lights illuminated the walls, making them glow and revealing mannequins adorned in some of the

Baroness's most stunning designs. These, Estella realized happily, were the Baroness's signature pieces. And they were right there–close enough to touch.

Opening another door, Estella and Jeffrey entered a large room encased in glass–the workroom. It was alive with activity. Seamstresses were sewing. Designers were sketching. Bolts of fabric were being wheeled in and out. Everywhere she looked there were images of clothes in various stages–from simple sketch to completed look. It was the most wondrous room Estella had ever stepped foot in.

Estella walked amid it all in a daze. Suddenly, she had a strange sensation, as if someone was watching her. She looked around. Everyone was focused on their work. Craning her head, she looked up, and her steps hesitated as she saw an office perched above them. It was surrounded by a balcony and seemed to somehow be floating above them.

Standing on the balcony, looking down at her, was the Baroness.

The Baroness watched as first Estella and then Jeffrey noticed her eyes on them. She wasn't often impressed by anyone—other than herself. But there had been something . . . inspiring in Estella's window display. Seeing it, the Baroness had made the hasty decision to hire her—mostly so she could keep an eye on this girl and prevent her from inspiring others with her own work. The Baroness prided herself on keeping ahead of any potential threats. And while Estella wasn't a threat yet, it was better to keep her underfoot. Her face neutral, the Baroness watched with a mixture of joy and pride as panic flooded the faces of her employees below. She waited for Jeffrey to do his job.

"Silence!" he shouted.

Instantly, all activity in the room stopped. No one moved. No one breathed. Well, no one except for one man who stood behind a cart of fabric, discreetly wheezing.

"I can hear breathing," the Baroness said.

"I've got asthma," the man said, trying to explain. "I . . ."

The Baroness simply raised an eyebrow. Instantly, the man sucked in his breath. While his face grew red, the Baroness turned and addressed everyone else. "My last show was a triumph. Shall I read from *Tattletale*?" Not bothering to wait for a response, she lifted a paper. Estella recognized the fashion section. She devoured it daily. "'Baroness designs stunned with her reinvention of the

A line, with a bias cut and higher line that reshapes the sil–'" On the floor below, the man with the asthma drew in a shaky, loud breath. The Baroness paused. Then, with a pointed frown, she went on. "'–houette in such an audacious way the audience broke into rapturous applause at first sight. She really is a genius.'" At the last word, the Baroness nodded, clearly in agreement. "Shall I read that last bit again? 'She really is a genius.'" She closed the paper. "A triumph. Again. Take a moment to revel in it."

For one brief second the employees seemed to relax. Smiles started to tug at their lips. The asthmatic man inhaled. The Baroness let them enjoy the moment. It would only make the next one more enjoyable to her. Just when she was sure all their heartbeats had returned to normal, the Baroness threw the paper down and the moment was over. "That's enough," she said. "New show. We must be perfect! Now go!" With orders dispatched, she did an about-face and headed back into her office.

Being the boss was such fun. Being the most frightening fashion boss was even better. As the Baroness settled back behind her desk, she allowed herself a smile. She really did love her life.

CHAPTER EIGHT

Estella didn't know what to do. The room was once again abuzz, but she wasn't sure what she was supposed to be buzzing over. Noticing her bewilderment, Jeffrey clapped his hands to get her attention.

"You–window girl," he said, "grab a mannequin, some fabric, and throw something together. The Baroness needs looks." With a curt nod, he bustled away.

That was it? Just throw something together? Estella hesitated, staring at the other designers busily working. They all seemed to have an idea in mind. But how long had they been working there? The looks they created could have taken weeks, years even, to create. She was supposed to just make one now? She didn't even know where to find the fabric.

Taking a deep breath, Estella straightened her shoulders. She hadn't made it this far without being quick on her feet. If the Baroness wanted a new look, Estella would make one. She spotted a doorway on the other side of the room and made her way through it. This was where she had seen the fabric come in; maybe there was more.

Sure enough, walking through the door, she found herself in a stairwell. Racks of fabrics lined the dark space. Even in the dim light, the colors were bright and bold. Estella smiled. This she could work with.

She began to gather her material. A yard here, a yard there. Chiffon, silk, denim. There was every type of fabric imaginable. Soon her arms were full, and she made her way back into the workroom.

For the next hour, Estella lost herself in her work. The sounds of the room faded away as she snipped and tucked, gathered and folded, sewed and pinned. She hadn't started out with a plan, but as always happened, with the material in her hand, a look began to materialize. For some reason, she had been drawn to the pink fabrics in the stairwell. Maybe it was because she was so used to using bland colors to blend in; maybe it was because she was in a good mood. Whatever the reason, bit by bit, the pinks came together, their slightly different shades blending into a dress that was both demure and demanding of attention.

Standing up to stretch, Estella realized that the room had grown quiet. Even as a recent hire, Estella knew that could mean only one thing: the Baroness was coming. The designers were now standing next to their mannequins, hands nervously clutched in front of them. Estella moved beside her mannequin and waited.

On cue, the Baroness entered the workroom. Without a word, she walked down the line of mannequins, eyeing them and assessing them instantly.

"Foolish," she noted to one. "Unhinged," she said to another. Stopping in front of a particularly outlandish design with elaborate beading and multiple fabrics sewn together: "You're fired."

Finally, she came to Estella's creation. Once again, the Baroness paused. Estella held her breath. She felt the other designers' eyes on her as the Baroness's eyes ran up and down the simple line of the dress, her head cocked. There was a pause that seemed to last for eternity.

"Not bad," the Baroness said.

Estella's breath was just about to whoosh out of her body when the Baroness pulled out a razor and, in one swift move, whipped it over the excess fabric. Estella had been going to get to that; she had just run out of time. Though she had to admit, as she looked at the Baroness's work, she would not have done such an amazing job. With a few quick flicks of the razor, the Baroness had formed the dress into a tighter, cleaner design. One more flick and the Baroness was done, though Estella winced as she was nicked in the process.

"Ow," she said softly, looking at her hand. A small red dot had appeared on it.

"Why are you speaking?" the Baroness responded.

Estella held up her hand. "Oh, sorry," she said. "I think you nicked me."

"Hmmm," the Baroness said, taking Estella's hand and lifting it to her face. She examined the drop of blood closely and shouted over her shoulder. "Fabric! Get me a red like this!" Then, without another word, she left.

Estella watched her go, her mind racing. The Baroness hadn't hated her design. True, but she hadn't said she loved it, either. At least she hadn't fired her.

So that was something . . . wasn't it?

Chapter 9

As Estella's tenure with the House of Baroness advanced, the days began to fall into a comfortable routine, or as comfortable as possible when one worked for a ruthless fashion designer who was prone to outbursts of anger and easily frustrated. Estella woke early and got to the warehouse before the others arrived. And from that moment until lunch, Estella was lost in her own world–sketching, designing, sewing, and mending. Every day brought a new bolt of fabric, a new spark of inspiration.

And then, just when Estella's stomach began to grumble, the Baroness made an appearance in the workroom. On the plus side, it usually scared away Estella's hunger, as the designers were encouraged to eat on their own time. On the downside, one could never guess what type of mood the Baroness would be in. Some days she was cold–which was her version of nice. Other days she was icy, and still others she was downright arctic. Still, as long as the woman kept inspiring her and offering her ways to improve, Estella would gladly take the moods.

So the days went on, and while she was never less than exhausted when she returned to the Lair each night, Estella had never been happier.

One late morning, Estella was just about to put the last touches on a design she had been sketching when she heard the unmistakable click of the Baroness's heels outside the workroom. Putting down her pen, she stood at attention. She glanced at the clock: it was 11:30 a.m. Yes, it was almost time for the Baroness to send someone for her lunch.

A moment later the Baroness appeared. As always, Jeffrey stood by her side. Her eyes traveled around the room and then stopped on Estella. "Grubby girl," she said. Estella looked down at her clothes. Did she mean her? But she had just cleaned her outfit the night before. Although her hands, she realized, were stained with ink. "Go get me lunch." The Baroness went on to place an impossible order for even the most seasoned of servers. Estella listened closely, trying to remember every detail. There were cucumber slices cut a certain width. A particular number of parsley sprigs and the express direction for them to be "shredded, not torn". When the Baroness was done, Estella nodded and quickly left. She needed to get the food before she forgot.

Luckily, the Baroness frequented the restaurant, so they were used to her particular "style" of ordering and didn't bat an eye when Estella articulated the order. She waited, growing nervous as the time seemed to drag. The Baroness hated to be kept waiting. When the food was finally finished, Estella raced back to the warehouse and bustled upstairs.

She stopped in front of the office door. It was open, but there were two men inside speaking to the Baroness. Her face was a mask. Estella hesitated.

"As the department stores that stock your range," one of the men was saying, "we thought perhaps we could give you some input."

The other man, wearing a suit and expression identical to his companion's, nodded in agreement. "Feedback."

The Baroness raised one perfectly plucked eyebrow. "Great," she said. The two men started to relax, but then she went on. "I'll start. My feedback. You're short, you're fat, you smell like an anchovy and are color-blind and pretend you aren't." The shorter of the two men shifted nervously in his seat, and Estella could have sworn he tried to smell himself. The Baroness turned to the other man. "Your revenues are down twelve and a half percent, foot traffic down fifteen." The man looked surprised to hear the figures. "Yes, I do my own research. Your store hasn't been refurbished since the Blitz; people aren't sure whether to buy or duck and cover."

Estella listened with a mixture of fear and fascination. She had never heard anyone speak in such a bold and confident way–let alone a woman. It was brilliant to watch, though Estella would never want to be at the other end of the lashing.

The Baroness wasn't done. "Most of the money meant for upgrades is being embezzled by you stashing it in a Swiss bank." She rattled off the exact account number as the men's faces paled. "Great. I'm done," she finally said, her tone satisfied, as she sat back in her chair. "Your turn. I'm all ears."

Quickly, the men got to their feet. "Good day," the taller one managed to mutter before he turned and hightailed it out of the office. The other suit followed. As they brushed past Estella, she was almost sure she heard one of them sniffling.

Just then the Baroness looked up. "Lunch!" she said, all vestiges of the previous exchange apparently forgotten. "Now!"

Estella hurried over and handed the Baroness her meal. She just hoped that it hadn't grown cold, or that the seven sprigs of shredded–not torn–parsley hadn't wilted in the meantime.

Leaning over, the Baroness examined her food as closely as she examined a design. Then she nodded. "Finally," she said, "someone competent."

Estella blushed at the compliment and was about to say thank you when there was a sound from the doorway. Turning, she watched a young man trip into the room. The Baroness sighed. "And someone not," she said. To Estella's surprise, the Baroness continued to address her directly. "This is Roger, my lawyer. Although he spends most of his time playing piano in a dingy bar."

"Hi," Roger said, lifting a hand filled with papers in greeting.

"Hi," Estella said. Then, when she realized she should say something more, she added, "Piano's nice."

Ignoring both of them, the Baroness picked two cucumbers from her lunch, and lying down on the chaise lounge in the corner of her office, she put them on her eyes. "Time for my nine-minute power nap," she said. "Estella, box up my lunch."

She knows my name! Estella thought as she quickly did as she was told. She hadn't heard the Baroness call any of the other women or men in the workroom by their real names. What could it mean? Had something just shifted?

Placing the rest of the food back in its container, Estella turned back to the Baroness. "Right," she said just as Roger said, "Could I just . . ."

But neither of them got a response. The Baroness was out cold.

Exchanging looks, Estella and Roger slowly crept out

of the room. Estella knew the saying–never wake a sleeping bear or risk its claws. If she had just had what could be considered, well, a *moment* with the Baroness, she wasn't going to risk a thing.

Estella was nervous. While the Baroness had continued to throw her scraps of attention, Estella was never sure when the attention might end. It made every request, every moment, every sketch fraught with tension. That morning was no different. Walking onto the balcony outside her office right before lunch, the Baroness had told, or rather ordered, Estella to go with her. Moments later, Estella had found herself sitting in the back of the Baroness's car. Nodding at the sketchbook Estella always carried with her, the Baroness had told her to rework an older sketch.

Relaxing back against the plush leather on the seat opposite Estella, the Baroness began to eat her lunch while Estella worked.

As they moved along the city streets, the car bounced over a pothole. The Baroness appeared personally offended by the condition of the streets. Her glance landed on the sketch pad in Estella's lap. "Maybe it needs a lining?" she said.

Estella cocked her head. That was an idea. "Could use some tulle to puff it out," she suggested, building off of the Baroness's thought. "Give it some body."

The Baroness nodded and took one last bite of her lunch, then threw the rest of it out the window. Catching Estella's surprised look, the Baroness shrugged. "For the neighbors," she said. "They hate me. Working woman. New money. So if they hate me anyway, I'll give them a reason." Spotting the gates to Ipswich Manor, she sat up. "Ah, here we are," she said.

As the car moved through a huge set of gates and up to the manor, Estella's eyes widened. On either side were immaculate plantings without a flower or leaf out of place. Even the gravel on the drive seemed to have been evened out so there was not a bump to be felt. But that all paled in comparison to the huge mansion. It had dozens of windows and was a full floor higher than any of the surrounding homes. Coming out the doors to greet them was a line of servants.

CHAPTER NINE

As the car stopped, the Baroness waved away the offer for a hand from her driver. She ignored the servants, too, and walked straight into the house, dropping gloves and her hat as she went. The two bodyguards, who were never far away, stayed close while a trio of Dalmatians bolted up to the Baroness, barking eagerly for attention. She ignored them. Behind her, Estella struggled to keep up, her eyes glued on the dogs. She normally considered herself a dog person–but Dalmatians did not count. Not since the night three of them had killed her mother. Eyeing the three standing beside the Baroness now, Estella forced down a wave of nausea.

They continued to sweep through the mansion, not stopping until they arrived at the Baroness's bedchambers. The room was bigger than the entire design space at the warehouse. The ceilings were twenty feet high, and the walls were covered in rich paper. Under her feet, the rug was plush.

Stopping in front of a full-length mirror, the Baroness waited as two of her maids entered and began to dress her. She stood like a living mannequin, her expression bored as she was tucked and shoved into her dress.

Estella began to sketch in her pad, taking inspiration from her surroundings as a new dress took shape on the page.

"Estella!" The Baroness's voice startled Estella and she flipped back to the image she had been sketching in the car. "The bodice. Maybe pencil thin. Jewels!" The Baroness turned her commanding voice to address John, her valet, ordering him to retrieve her priceless accessories. The man moved toward the far wall of the room. He pushed on the wall, and a secret door slid open, revealing another locked door behind that. The guard pulled out a key and unlocked the door, then disappeared inside.

"Did you do pencil thin?" the Baroness asked, returning her attention to Estella.

Estella nodded but didn't answer, focused on refining the design. A moment later, the valet reappeared from the hidden room with a tray of sparkling jewels in his hands. The Baroness stepped off the pedestal she had been standing on and walked over. Absently, she rifled through the diamonds and sapphires, rubies and emeralds. She pushed aside a few smaller pieces before finally picking a diamond set that included a necklace, earrings, and a huge ring.

"All right," she said, presenting herself to the room. "How do I look?"

"Fabulous," everyone in the room replied without hesitation.

The Baroness seemed barely to register the canned compliment. "Estella," she said. "Show me."

Quickly, Estella made her way over. Holding out the sketch pad, she showed the woman the design she had dictated. The Baroness nodded curtly. "How would you have done it?"

Estella paused. She was unsure what to say. Did the Baroness actually want Estella to contradict her design, or was this a trap? After a moment's thought, Estella took a risk and made some quick amendments to the design, handing it over with bated breath.

The Baroness stared at the paper for a long moment. "I think you're . . . something," the Baroness finally said. Then, without another word, she turned and left the room, her minions following.

Chapter 10

Estella's eyes hurt. She had been staring at a design sketch pinned to the wall of the Baroness's office for nearly an hour, trying to "make it better". Beside her, the Baroness sat at her desk, pointing out flaw after flaw. Each time, Estella would sketch something better and pin it up for comparison. She didn't mind the critique. It only made her a stronger designer. And while she didn't exactly like the Baroness, she definitely respected her eye. So she put up with the comments and the sharp remarks.

CHAPTER TEN

"There's something irritating me about it," the Baroness said now, looking at the latest design. "And I always trust my instincts."

Estella quickly did another sketch and pinned it to the wall. "I thought maybe tighten the silhouette?" she suggested.

"Oh, you 'thought', did you?" the Baroness said.

Estella nodded toward the new sketch She was more confident in her role with the Baroness. But she had never been bold enough to contradict her. Until now. "I think that's better," she affirmed, sticking with her gut.

For a moment, the room filled with a tense silence and Estella bit her lip. But then, to her surprise–and delight–the Baroness nodded. "Actually, it is," she agreed. As she spoke, the Baroness turned in her seat just as a ray of light came through the skylight, illuminating the delicate necklace the Baroness was wearing that day.

Estella let out a small gasp.

It was her mum's necklace–the one she had lost on that horrible night years earlier.

Until that moment, Estella hadn't noticed it. It had been hidden behind the scarf draped stylishly around the

Baroness's neck. But now it was there, flashing in front of Estella's face and making her feel sick.

Why, Estella thought, trying to keep her hands from shaking, was it now on the Baroness's neck?

"Your necklace," Estella said, her voice trembling.

The Baroness took a thin slice of cucumber off the plate in front of her, not acknowledging the emotion in Estella's face or the look of disbelief in her eyes. "Family heirloom," she said dismissively. "Funny story, actually. An employee stole it."

"No, she did *not*!" The words were out of Estella's mouth before she could stop herself.

Looking up, the Baroness gave Estella a cold stare. Pushing back on designs was one thing, but no one talked to her that way.

Recovering, Estella gave the woman a deferential smile, even as her mind was whirring. How had she not put it together sooner?

The Baroness. The woman whose party she and her mum had intruded on years earlier. The woman who had three large Dalmatians.

They were the same person.

Estella had been young, and the night was shadowed in such misery that she must have blocked out what the woman looked like. But now it all came rushing back. The woman, standing at the top of the steps, dressed like Marie Antoinette, and then later watching passively as her mother fell. The sound of dogs barking and Estella's silent scream.

Estella forced her mind back to the present. "Sorry. Slight tone delivery problem. It's a question like 'No! She did not?!' She worked for you?" she said, hoping that sounded at all believable.

Apparently, it had, as the Baroness nodded. "Once," she said. "Years before that. Stole this from me, and was dumb enough to come back. Then she fell off a cliff and died."

"How terrible?" Estella said weakly. Bile rose in her throat. How could the Baroness refer to her mother's death so casually?

"It was during my winter ball, and her death really overshadowed the whole thing." The Baroness stretched and yawned. "Okay, I need my nine-minute power nap. Wake me when I'm done."

Estella nodded. "Will do," she said, voice chipper. She

stared at the Baroness. It was taking everything she had not to walk over and hit the woman across her smug face. Her mother's death, which had left Estella orphaned, was an *inconvenience*? To her party? Taking a deep breath, she centered her anger. She couldn't change the past. But she could try to get some answers to questions she had asked herself countless times over the years.

"Who was the woman to you?" Estella asked, keeping her tone deliberately casual.

"Not really the point of the story," the Baroness said, making her way to her chaise. "Was more about how lucky I am. She had a kid, kid's a snowflake, special, blah blah, was a basic shakedown situation."

Estella gritted her teeth. That was not what it was at all. "Maybe she just loved her kid?"

"Maybe she only had one person to take care of and she failed dismally," the Baroness retorted.

Estella felt the words like a slap. Her mum had loved her and sacrificed everything for her. And the Baroness was talking about her like she was trash.

Unaware of Estella's inner turmoil, the Baroness lay down and placed the cucumbers over her eyes. A moment later, she was snoring.

Estella stared down at her, eyes locked on the necklace. It was so close. If she just reached out . . .

Suddenly, from out in the hall, she heard voices coming closer. A moment later Jeffrey and Roger entered the office, followed by two harried assistants carrying a beautiful gown. Behind them came the bodyguards. John was holding the Baroness's travel box of jewels. Upon spotting Estella, he gave her a hard stare.

"Baroness," Roger said softly. "We have that meeting at the Ritz . . ."

Muttering a few choice words under her breath, the Baroness peeled herself off the chaise. Her nine-minute nap had been less than five. She was going to be crankier than normal. Standing, the Baroness remained silent as two nervous maids dressed and pampered her. Finally, her dress fastened and her hair done, the Baroness gestured for the jewelry box.

Peering inside, she picked out a new necklace and removed the one around her neck. Estella's eyes stayed glued to her mum's necklace as it was dropped unceremoniously into the box. John watched her watching, his eyes widening slightly, not with suspicion so much as something different–like understanding. Then he snapped the box shut.

A moment later, the Baroness strutted out of the office, her entourage following.

Estella watched them go. Her feet were frozen to the floor. She had spent so much time trying to prove herself to the Baroness. She had put all her hopes and dreams into working for the woman.

And she was a monster.

A monster who didn't care that Estella's mum had died or that a young girl had been left orphaned. A monster who only cared about herself and her stupid party.

Estella's broken dream tasted like ash in her mouth.

What, she wondered, her heart breaking once again, *am I going to do now?*

Estella wasn't ready to go back to the Lair. But she didn't want to stay in the warehouse any longer. Seeing the Baroness's name on every item of clothing, every sketch on the wall, every paper in the bin just made her ill.

She grabbed her things and walked out of the warehouse. In a fog, she made her way along the streets, not thinking about where she was going. She just let her feet take her as her mind went back to that dark night years earlier. She hadn't thought about it in so long. But now it was as clear as if it had just happened.

Her mum and the Baroness talking. The dogs barking. And then her mum, gone. Lost over the cliff to the water below.

For years Estella had lived with the consequences, forced to find a home on the streets. And during that same time, the Baroness had lounged about in her fancy mansion going to the best parties, creating fantastic designs, and making her name synonymous with high fashion.

It wasn't fair.

Sighing, Estella looked up and saw that she had made her way into Regent's Park. The fountain seemed to glow in the bright light from the moon. Estella walked to a nearby bench, sinking down onto its hard surface and putting her head in her hands.

Sensing eyes on her, Estella looked up. To her surprise, she saw Jasper and Horace. They were standing in front of her. Jasper looked concerned. Horace looked, well, like Horace.

"Told you," Horace said smugly. "She always comes here."

Estella shrugged. He wasn't wrong. But why had they been looking for her? She glanced up at the darkening sky and remembered. They were supposed to be pulling a job that evening down in the theater district. She hadn't realized how late it had become. Suddenly, her eyes welled and a torrent of words rushed from her mouth.

"She called my mum a thief," Estella said. "Said she failed as a mother."

Jasper shook his head, trying to process what Estella was saying and who Estella was talking about. Then his eyes widened as he figured it out. "The Baroness knew your mum?"

Estella nodded. Getting to her feet, she rubbed her palms down the front of her shirt, composing herself. "Turns out it was her party we were at, all those years ago," she explained. "Mum worked for her once. I dropped the necklace as I ran away. She must have found it." Saying the words out loud made the situation seem even more real and more horrible. But they also gave Estella new determination toward what she knew would be her inevitable next step, ever since the moment she saw the necklace. She had no other choice. "I'm taking it back."

"Taking it?" Jasper repeated. "As in . . . ?"

"Stealing it," Estella finished. That was exactly what she was going to do. The Baroness was not going to get to keep the one remaining thing of Estella's mum. "I could ask for it, but she's kind of a horrible person, so she probably wouldn't give it back. And stealing it is way more fun anyway." She smiled as Horace nodded in obvious agreement.

"Finally!" he said happily. "The angle!"

"She's got a lot of jewelry," Estella said to Horace. "You can take it all. Follow your dreams. One last job."

Jasper shrugged. He didn't want one last job. He was quite happy with his life. "But lots of jewels are always good," he agreed.

Horace had no hesitation. "Sounds high class," he said, puffing out his large belly, "and that's me all over."

Throwing her arms around these men who had become her makeshift family, Estella gave them a squeeze. True, they weren't biologically related, but they had her back . . . always. And now they were going to help her take back what was rightfully hers.

All they needed was a plan.

Chapter 11

Estella had always loved the planning part of the trio's heists. It was fun, a good distraction, and a way to feel like she had some control over her life. Now it was business. She wanted to get that necklace back—and if the Baroness suffered a bit along the way, so be it. She had hurt Estella; now Estella would hurt her back.

Fortunately, Estella had come to learn that the Baroness was a creature of habit. She started every morning with the same meal. She had lunch from the same three spots. Her nine-minute power nap occurred every day exactly thirteen minutes after her last bite of lunch. Her bodyguards never changed, because if they did, she would have to train a new pair and that would cost her time, and time, as she reminded everyone, was money.

So life for the Baroness was routine.

That was just what Estella wanted.

Reconnaissance began almost immediately. Walking into the warehouse the next morning, Estella felt as if she were seeing it for the first time. She was no longer looking at it as a place to create fashion, form ideas. Instead, it was a mark.

She kept an eye on when the bodyguards arrived. She noted what, if anything, distracted them. Sitting in the Baroness's office, she noted that John, the valet, always kept a hand near the large key ring he wore looped on his belt.

"No chance I'm going to get the necklace there," Estella told the boys after her first day of surveillance. "We're going to need to go for it where she would least expect it–at her house."

There was just one problem: Ipswich Manor was

almost as heavily fortified as the warehouse. The Baroness took no chances. She had cameras. She had guards. She had the dogs. But Estella had worked as a thief long enough to know that every camera had a blind spot. Every security guard had a weakness. And every dog—well, dogs could be bribed . . . she hoped.

"You have to get us as much intel as you can," Jasper said one night as Estella plotted and fumed. She had wanted this to be a quick job. In, out. Get the necklace and get away from the Baroness. But it was proving to be much more complicated.

Still, she knew that Jasper was right. The more information they had, the better prepared they would be. So while the Baroness took a power nap in her bedroom one afternoon, Estella snuck out and did a sweep of the halls. If a random guard spotted her, she made an excuse about looking for the bathroom even as she kept an eye on the clock. Nine minutes wasn't a lot of time, but after several days, she thought she had enough.

Standing in front of a wall at the Lair, Estella reviewed the gathered intel. The wall had become mission control: there were lists of names, blueprints to the manor, dates circled in red, pictures of all the guards, and a list of the dogs' favorite treats. In the middle of it all was an invitation, lengths of string linking it to a dozen other pieces of information.

"Her Black and White Ball," Estella said, turning to look at the boys. "That's where we'll do it." She had taken her time making the decision. The house would be at capacity. The necklace would be tucked away in the safe where the Baroness kept all her jewels. The guards would be looking out for intruders, not thinking to look in–and especially not thinking to look at Estella. After all, she had proved her loyalty. Or so they thought.

"It's our biggest job ever," Jasper said, taking off his hat and holding it nervously to his chest.

Estella nodded. He was right. Which meant their planning had to be meticulous. They all needed to be on the exact same page. She looked down and saw that Horace was lying on a pile of papers. She sighed.

"Disable the security system," she said, thinking out loud. "Bypass the cameras. Open the safe. Steal the necklace." It sounded simple enough.

"Get out without being seen," Horace pointed out from the floor.

Yes, there was that.

But that was why Estella had chosen the ball. It made for a perfect cover. "During the biggest party of the season?" she said, shaking off his concern. "So many people we can get lost in the sea. And then when we need it, a distraction where I get the key for the keypad and the safe."

It seemed simple enough to Estella. But looking at Jasper, she saw his brows were furrowed. That was never a good thing. It meant he was thinking. And if he was thinking, he was probably finding holes in her plan.

Estella was right. Jasper had been thinking. And listening. He was impressed with Estella's attention to detail and the plan that she had concocted. But he was also a little nervous. There were so many variables. And part of their success came from keeping the jobs manageable. This one seemed huge—and far too personal.

Walking to the wall that had become the trio's makeshift mission control, Jasper stared at its contents like they alone could give him the answers. "What's the distraction?"

"I've discovered that she likes to throw women who

offend her sensibilities out of her parties: old women, sad women, women in green, women who carry poodles," Estella explained. "But also, stunningly dressed women who pull the focus off her."

Jasper nodded. So that was how Estella was going to get to the Baroness–and the necklace.

"So we need to find one of them," Horace mused, catching on. Jasper shot him a smile. Even though his friend could be slow to catch on, he usually did–just at his own speed. "The old woman seems easiest."

To his surprise, Estella rolled her eyes. That wasn't like her. But then again, she hadn't been herself since she found out the truth. He was trying to be understanding, but there were moments, like now, when her attitude made him uncomfortable. Horace was her friend. He was family. He wasn't always speedy, but Jasper knew Horace would be there for her.

"Me," she said, collecting herself. "I'm going to be the distraction." She smiled. "Mayhem, destruction, death . . . it's my specialty."

Jasper cocked his head and shot Estella a funny look. She shifted under his gaze, clearly uncomfortable. He knew she had been joking. But the death part? That was a bit much.

For a moment, he thought about correcting her, but then he shrugged. "Here's the problem," he said instead. "Won't she recognize you?"

Horace nodded in agreement. "That is a problem."

Estella shrugged. "I guess," she said.

"And won't you lose your job when that happens?" Jasper pointed out. "A job I think you love."

"A job he got you," Horace added, earning looks from both Estella and Jasper. For someone who seemed to never be following along, he was often spot-on.

Estella lowered her eyes, and Jasper knew that Horace had struck a nerve. He couldn't imagine what she was going through or what she was feeling. They hadn't been there that night. They hadn't watched the Baroness coldly turn her back on Estella's mum. And they hadn't been there in the office when she had just brushed off what happened as a mere inconvenience. He knew that this was about more than the necklace. But he also knew Estella wouldn't say that. And even if Jasper–and Horace–was right, she had worked too hard on all the recon and planning to back out now. There was only going to be a small window of time when the necklace would be accessible in the safe.

Lifting her head, Estella steeled her expression. "I want it back," she said. Jasper winced at the hardness in her voice.

"What she says goes," Horace said, shrugging.

Estella nodded and then turned to look at the wall. Jasper was right. While Estella wouldn't give him the satisfaction of acknowledging how much she loved the job she was about to lose, she couldn't deny that the Baroness would recognize her. Unless . . .

"Estella can't go to the ball," she said. "But I know someone who can."

Estella's long legs carried her swiftly down the London street. Her head moved back and forth as she scanned the shopwindows.

Estella's steps slowed as she passed by a vintage clothing shop. Standing front and center in the window display was a mannequin dressed in a stunning evening gown, matched with a wild jacket and neon pops of color. It was wickedly fun and vibrant and alive—just Estella's style.

Quickly, she walked into the store. A bell jingled as the door opened and shut behind her. The tiny space was full of racks of all types of clothes: brightly colored tops, flowered pants, maxi dresses, short dresses, tall boots, high heels, neon headbands. Every style from what seemed the last three decades was piled, hung, or dumped around the space.

Estella loved it.

A tall man with hair perfectly coiffed into a Bowie-style pompadour was perched on a chair, hitting the broken air conditioner, but he stopped what he was doing at the sound of the bells and turned toward Estella. His face was painted with a big bolt of lightning. Clearly, he was a fan of all things Ziggy Stardust.

"Welcome to Second Time Around. I'm Artie," he said cheerfully. "Or Art. As in a work of art."

Estella nodded. "You do look incredible," she said. And he did. The makeup was perfect—down to the subtle eye shadow that made his eyes pop and the blush on his cheeks that made them stand out. He had treated his face like a canvas and the result was stunning.

"I hear that all day," he said with a shrug. "So I guess it's true."

"How does that look go on the street?" she asked curiously.

"Some abuse and insults of course," Artie replied matter-of-factly. "But I like to say normal is the cruelest of all insults, and at least I never get that."

Estella smiled. She had clearly found a kindred spirit in Artie. From the display window to what Artie wore, he spoke her fashion language through and through. She had a feeling they were going to get along just fine.

"I need a gown," she said, cutting to the chase. "For a ball. And it needs to make an impact."

Artie gestured to the room around them. "Well, look around, Cinderella," he said happily. "I have everything a girl or boy could ever want. If you can dream it, I can dress it."

Estella began to peruse the racks like a kid in a candy store. Artie was right. He did have everything she could ever want or dream up. Dior '56. Chanel '32. Black gowns, white gowns, bright gowns. It was hard to pick which she loved most. But her eye kept going back to the red dress in the window.

"Baroness '65," Artie said, noticing her glance. "Winter collection."

Estella nodded. "I noticed that," she said. "And I call that fate."

Red.

Since she was a girl and had met Jasper and Horace, Estella had been dyeing her hair the same shade of box red. For most people, it would have been a bold color choice. But given Estella's natural locks, it felt safe to her. Now, though, it had to go.

Standing over the sink, she let the water run until it was lukewarm—which was about as warm as it ever got in the Lair. Watching as the water swirled down the drain, Estella took a deep breath. She was about to change something that had defined her for years. When she had first dyed her hair, she had been grieving. Her mum was gone. She had no home. She had only just met Jasper and Horace. Hiding who she really was didn't feel wrong. On the contrary, it felt necessary.

But in the years since, she had grown to love the red. It was who she was now; a departure from who she had been then. Still, if she was going to pull off her plan to retrieve her necklace and have even a shot of doing so unrecognized, getting rid of the red seemed like the best solution.

Dipping her hair under the flow, she watched as red dye swirled down the drain. The water gradually faded from bright red to pink and then to clear. When she stood up, the woman staring back in the mirror was at once familiar and a stranger.

Estella gave her reflection a nod. It was done.

Now it was time for action.

Chapter 12

The first part of the plan relied on Horace and Jasper. This had made Horace quite pleased but, he noticed, made Estella rather nervous.

To be safe, she had gone over the plan with them multiple times. Horace knew what they were supposed to do. His dog, Wink, also knew what he was supposed to do. Estella was on a mission to get that necklace, and if she wanted it, she was going to have to trust him.

Jasper pulled the exterminator truck up behind a line of cars in front of Ipswich Manor. Sitting in the passenger seat, Horace watched as, one by one, richly dressed guests were helped out of their cars and up to the front door. Each guest was dressed in either pure white or pure black. In Horace's opinion, it made everyone look pretty much the same, and that seemed pretty boring. In his lap, Wink whined. The dog didn't like being away from Buddy, but Estella had insisted on keeping Buddy with her for the main event. It was probably better. One dog was easier to watch over than two.

Amid the sea of black-and-white swankiness, Jasper and Horace's exterminator truck stood out like a big green sore thumb.

Jasper pulled the truck over and came to a stop away from the line of cars and right over a manhole cover. He put the truck in park. While Horace jumped out, Jasper crawled under the truck and lifted open the manhole. He would wait there until Horace gave him the all clear signal. Then he would hightail it to the security room and begin his part of the plan.

Giving Wink a reassuring pat, Horace watched the little dog race ahead of him. Then he took a deep breath and headed toward the service entrance. "I came as quick as I could," he said, coming to a stop in front of the security guard. "This is a private event," the guard responded in a toneless voice.

"Kind of vermin I deal with don't wait for an invitation, mate." He lowered his voice and leaned in, as if offering up a secret. "They get in, bite posh people, who first froth at the mouth. Then their eyes spin back in their heads, then they die. Then the guard who didn't do nothing about it . . . well . . . he is finished."

The security guard shook his head. "That's a beautiful story, mate," he said insincerely. "But I'm not buying it."

That was exactly what Horace had expected the man to say. It set up the next part of the plan brilliantly. As Horace had been telling his "beautiful story", Wink had slipped past the guard's feet and gotten in position. Now it was time for Horace to amp up the drama. His eyes widened as he looked at "something" behind the guard. "Freeze!" he said, dropping his voice so he sounded scared. "Whatever you do, don't turn around–"

Of course, the guard immediately turned around. From a shelf inside the doorway, Wink leapt out and, snarling, attached himself to the guard's face. The big man let out a piercing shriek as Wink gave one last growl and then raced off into the house.

"What are you standing there for?" the security guard shouted, turning to Horace. He hadn't gotten a good look at the dog, so he assumed the little creature was one of the vermin Horace had been warning him about. "Get it out!"

Horace nodded. While the guard stared nervously down the hall, Horace signaled to Jasper, who slipped down into the manhole. Then, turning to the guard, Horace added, "You better wash your hands."

With a wave, he sauntered into the house. He knew that somewhere in the tunnels below, Jasper was making his way to the basement to set up his computer equipment. In moments, he would have gained access to the closed-circuit feed and begun a loop on the cameras. The security guards would be looking at old footage. They would be virtually blind.

The whole thing had taken less than three minutes. And now Jasper and Horace had access to the entire manor. Everything was in place for Estella's arrival.

Anita Darling was furious at her boss. She had begged him not to make her cover the Baroness's Black and White Ball. She couldn't afford it–literally and figuratively. Looking down at her cheap knockoff dress, she repressed a groan. Even cheap, it had cost her more than a week's pay.

At twenty-five, Anita had hoped to have already had her big break in journalism. She had hoped to be writing about pressing issues, or at least getting front-page spreads. But she was still writing fashion pieces for *Tattletale*. Events like that night's ball, which required all attendees to don white or black–and only white or black–were what their readership ate up, but they ate Anita's soul bit by bit.

Pulling out her camera, appropriately covered in white to fit the theme, Anita snapped a few photos of the crowd and the decorations. They were, in her opinion, both over the top and rather gaudy. She hadn't thought it possible for the fashion-forward to make a mistake, but somehow she just couldn't wrap her head around the Baroness's vision. It was bland and seemed uninspired. As she turned to capture a woman wearing what appeared to be white lizard skin, Anita saw the Baroness descending the staircase into the main room. The Baroness spotted Anita at the same time and made her way over.

"Miss Anita Darling," the Baroness said in a voice that dripped with condescension.

"Baroness!" Anita said, forcing a smile on her face. "I'm

so grateful you've given *Tattletale* an exclusive tonight."

The Baroness looked Anita up and down. Anita flushed under the scrutiny. "Not, apparently," the Baroness said, "grateful enough to observe the dress code." Plucking Anita's white purse from her hand, the Baroness held it up. Anita grimaced. There was a tiny spot of blue ink near the bottom of the bag.

"My pen must have leaked," Anita said, laughing nervously. "Tools of the trade . . ."

"No one is interested in what you write, my dear," the Baroness said. "Just in how I look." With that, she turned and made her way into the crowd of people eagerly waiting to adore her. As she passed an ice bucket, the Baroness dropped Anita's offending purse inside.

Anita hated that the Baroness was right. No one cared what she wrote as long as there was a picture of the Baroness to go with it. *It would be nice if someone other than the Baroness got some attention for once,* she thought as she pulled her bag out of the ice.

But it was the Baroness's party. How could that ever happen?

Estella took a breath and steeled herself. She had planned this all out. She had gone down every possible avenue, envisioned every scenario. Plans had been checked and rechecked.

So then why, she wondered, did she feel so nervous?

True, if she got caught, she could get arrested. If she was recognized, she could lose her job. And if both happened? Well, she imagined she would get arrested and fired. It would all be worth it, though–if she could get her hands on that necklace.

With one more deep breath, she steadied her racing heart and walked through the front door and into the throng of partygoers. Her floor-length white coat covered her dress, while the hood covered her hair. As she ducked and weaved among the guests, hidden in plain sight, she smiled. So far, so good.

Under her arm, protected from view by Estella's cloak, Buddy wriggled. She gave him a gentle squeeze and then slid him to the floor. He quickly disappeared under a nearby table. When she was sure he was safe, Estella made her way over to another table near the center of the room. On top was a tower of champagne glasses. Balanced carefully

Estella's mum drops Estella off for her first day as a student at a fancy private school.

School isn't what Estella thought it would be—but she finds a new friend in a dog she names Buddy.

Years later, Jasper and Horace surprise Estella on her birthday with a job at Liberty of London department store, to help make her fashion designer dreams come true.

Estella decides to put her own spin on a window display in Liberty of London.

Baroness Von Hellman, creator of House of Baroness fashion, sees Estella's work at Liberty and offers her a job as a designer.

Estella begins to consider a plot to take down the Baroness, with the help of Jasper and Horace.

Estella goes undercover as Cruella for the first time at the Baroness's Black and White Ball.

Horace and Wink go undercover at the ball.

Jasper and Horace dognap the Baroness's prized trio of Dalmatians.

Cruella makes a splash and spoils the Baroness's grand entrance at a red-carpet event.

Anita, a friend from Estella's childhood and a reporter for *Tattletale*, captures all of Cruella's appearances, making her famous.

Jasper and Horace help Estella wreck the Baroness's fashion show—and put on a show all Cruella's own.

Jasper plays the guitar at Cruella's pop-up fashion show.

Cruella proves she is here to stay.

Jasper and Horace find themselves in some trouble after helping Cruella with her fashion show.

Cruella ruins the Baroness once and for all.

upon their thin stems, the glasses glimmered and sparkled with the liquid gold inside.

Estella watched as a waiter came and refilled his tray with glasses. He turned and moved to distribute them among the guests as the Baroness headed over to stand on the stairs. Looking out, she waited for the room to grow quiet. Hushed anticipation fell over the crowd. Estella took a step closer to the champagne tower. She, too, waited.

The Baroness was clearly loving the moment. She dragged it out, letting all eyes rest on her and her beautiful gown. She preened, turning and shifting so that every angle of her dress could be seen, every exquisite element highlighted. Estella heard the sound of a camera clicking rapidly and glanced toward it. A woman about her age was snapping up pictures as fast as her thumb would allow. Estella held in a groan. Of course. The Baroness wasn't just acting like she was on display, she *was* on display—or would be when tomorrow's edition of *Tattletale* came out.

But there will be more to the story, Estella thought wickedly as she turned back to the stairs.

"Here's to me!" the Baroness said, finally raising her glass in the air.

The crowd did the same. Glasses were brought to lips. Mouths were opened. And then . . . *crash*!

The sound of a hundred champagne glasses falling to the floor echoed through the huge room. Instantly, all heads turned from the Baroness–and landed on Estella.

Standing next to the now destroyed champagne tower, Estella shrugged, as if to say "Oops!"

With everyone looking at her, no one but Estella noticed Horace and Wink, now dressed as a rat, enter the room through the service door. Good, things were still on schedule. Casting her eyes around the ladies and gentlemen near her, Estella nodded to an older man. He looked a bit fragile and frightened, and for a moment, Estella felt bad for what was to come. But then she shrugged it off. "Do you have a light?" she asked coquettishly.

He nodded and fumbled in his jacket pocket until he pulled out a matchbook. There was a spark as the match lit. Handing it to Estella, he hesitated, unsure what she needed it for, as she wasn't holding a cigarette.

Upon taking it from him, Estella smiled and promptly dropped the match–right on her cloak.

With a whoosh, the white fabric of the cloak and hood

disintegrated in a sheet of flame. The fire quickly faded, revealing the bloodred gown beneath and Estella's black-and-white hair. Lifting her eyes, Estella met the Baroness's gaze.

Checkmate, she thought as the Baroness, trying to keep her cool, gave her two security guards a hard look. "I want her," Estella heard her hiss.

"Alive?" the bigger of the two guards asked.

The Baroness nodded. "For now."

"This doesn't have to be a scene," he warned Estella when he reached her.

Estella smiled. "Oh, but it does," she said. "It really, really does."

Not pleased with her response, the guard went to grab Estella's arm. In a flash, she brought down the cane she was holding onto his hand and then, raising her voice so everyone could hear, she called out, "Ow! My arm! It may be broken!" Just as she anticipated, the guests began to mutter nervously. She kept at it. "I think it is. Is there a doctor in the house?" For added effect, she let her hand drop limply by her side.

By now everyone was staring at Estella. They were

confused–and rightly so. Why, they wondered, would the Baroness be that upset? The girl had knocked over the champagne tower. It was just an accident . . .

Estella, however, had expected nothing less. She could feel the Baroness's cold eyes on her even as the guards came ever closer. Suddenly, one lunged at her. Estella dodged the move swiftly, ducking down and then swiping her cane across his legs so that he tripped and tumbled to the floor. Knocked momentarily out of breath, he struggled on the floor. This was Estella's chance. Leaning over, she muttered a fake apology–as she picked the man's pocket. Rising up, she smiled to the captive audience. "I'd like to point out I'm doing all this in heels," she said lightly. Then she flipped her cane up in the air and let it twirl. As it did, she watched the keys, which she had smoothly placed on the bottom of the cane, fly off and up through the air. On the balcony, Horace reached out his hand and snagged them, no one any the wiser.

Estella met his eyes as the cane came back to her hand. She nodded. Good, another step smoothly executed. But then she saw Horace lift a walkie-talkie to his ear and listen. A nervous look crossed his face. There must be a problem with the video loop that they had set up to keep prying eyes from watching the safe room. Their plan hinged on getting into that safe room. Estella had checked and rechecked during her recon. The Baroness never left her jewelry out. It always went in the safe. There was no way the Baroness would wear Catherine's cheap necklace at an event like that night's. It had to be in the safe. That meant the only reason Jasper would be talking to Horace was if the loop had been broken. The security guards would be able to see what was going on. That wasn't good. They needed the guards to be blind.

Sure enough, a moment later, Horace shouted. It looked like they were going with plan B.

While Horace frantically sprayed Wink with fake vermin spray and Jasper, hidden from view, worked his magic fixing the cameras, Estella thought quickly. She needed to give Horace time to get into the room with the safe.

Turning back, she saw that more guards had appeared. She was surrounded. There was nowhere to go. Or so it would seem. "So obviously," Estella said, putting on as much confidence as she could muster, given the odds, "there's six of you, so you'll win. But the first two of you to arrive are going to be very badly hurt. So decide amongst yourselves who that is."

There was a pause as the men weighed her words. Then, with a shrug, one of them approached her from behind and grabbed her shoulder. In a flash, Estella raised her cane and walloped him in the face. As that guard groaned, another came at her. Once again wielding her cane like a sword, she struck him in the chest and, with another flick of her wrist, whacked him in his chin. "Is that two?" she asked, starting to enjoy herself. "I lost count."

Spinning again, she raised her cane to take out the next guard. The man's eyes met hers as her hand came down. With practiced skill, he raised his own hand–and caught the cane midair. Estella grunted as he tugged her to him, capturing her arms and pinning them to her sides.

From across the room, the Baroness nodded. "Bring her to me," she ordered.

Dragging her over, the guard shoved Estella in front of the Baroness. Estella froze. This close, she was sure that the Baroness would recognize her. She stared at the older woman, and then she saw her mum's necklace hanging around the Baroness's neck. *Well,* she thought as the Baroness told everyone to go back to the party, *that was a twist I didn't see coming.*

Chapter 13

"Who are you?" the Baroness asked Estella as she glided away from the stairs and toward a small alcove. "You look vaguely familiar."

"I look stunning," Estella said, relieved. The Baroness hadn't recognized her—yet. Quickly, she fell into the role of mysterious fashionista that she had perfected during her long hours of prep. "I don't know about familiar, darling."

The Baroness looked almost impressed by the response.

Almost. Narrowing her eyes, she nodded at Estella's head. "Your hair, is it real?"

"Black and White Ball," Estella replied, not giving a definitive answer. "I like to make an impact."

"Right," the Baroness said, unconvinced. "What was your name?"

Estella felt her heart begin to pound faster. She hadn't thought of that. She couldn't just come out and say her name. But she couldn't just stand there gasping like a fish on dry land. Her brain whirred as she tried to come up with an alias. Her eyes stayed locked on the Baroness's cold ones. There was something so mean and vindictive in them. It reminded her of the ginger boy who had made her life horrible in grade school. And just like that, she knew exactly the name she would give the Baroness.

"Cruella," Estella answered boldly.

For the first time since Estella had known the Baroness, she saw what looked like approval cross over the woman's face. "That's quite fabulous," the Baroness said. "And you designed this?" She pointed toward the red gown.

"You did. In your 1965 collection," Estella replied.

She paused for a beat, letting the words sink in. Then she added, "I fixed it."

The Baroness leveled her gaze at Estella. For a long moment, the two women stood in a silent face-off. Then the Baroness nodded. "No wonder I love it. It's mine," she said, ignoring Estella's comment. "I don't recall inviting you."

"Neither do I," Estella said. Her earlier tension was fading as she slipped further and further into her new role. "And yet, here I am."

The Baroness walked over and took a seat in the larger of two chairs placed in the alcove. It had a high back and stiff padding. A throne, Estella thought, for an ice queen. Pointing to the smaller chair beside hers, the Baroness told her to sit. "I insist," she said. "I'm intrigued, and that never happens."

As Estella moved toward the chair, the Baroness's three Dalmatians approached. Instantly, Estella's blood ran cold. The dogs were huge, each one bigger than the last. She tried to slow her breath as she remembered, in a terrible flash, a blur of black and white coming at her as she hid behind a hedge. These couldn't be the same dogs that had attacked her mother, could they? Did the Baroness just replace one dog with the next, like a handbag?

Mistaking Estella's look of fear for admiration, the Baroness called one of the dogs over and placed her long, thin fingers atop its head. "Aren't they gorgeous?" the Baroness said. "And vicious. It's my favorite combination."

Gulping, Estella inched by the dogs and slid into the seat. As she did so, the dogs let out low growls, almost in recognition.

"Now, what do you want?" the Baroness asked, handing Estella a glass of champagne. Taking her own, she sipped at the golden bubbles, her eyes never leaving Estella. "You obviously wanted to get my attention."

Estella took a sip of her own drink. She had hoped to stay at a distance from the Baroness. "I guess," she said, adlibbing, "I'd love to know your secret."

The Baroness nodded, as if expecting that. "Two hours sleep a night," she began. "Rule with fear, be a creative genius, let nothing stand in your way, and destroy all and any competition . . ."

As the Baroness spoke, Estella spotted Buddy. The dog had slipped to the alcove unnoticed and was now hiding under the side table between their chairs. Estella shot a glance toward the Dalmatians. Luckily, they hadn't picked up Buddy's scent, but it was only a matter of time.

"Which makes me wonder," the Baroness continued. "Are you competition, Cruella?"

Estella's head snapped up. "Trick question," she replied. "If I say, I might destroy me. Perhaps I'm a new friend?"

The Baroness gave Estella a patronizing smile. "I don't have friends, dear," she said simply.

"How lonely for you."

The Baroness shook her head. "I just can't find someone who reaches my standards, so I prefer it." She paused and took a sip of her drink. "And you? What do you want?"

The question surprised Estella and she hesitated, trying to think of an answer. As she thought, she glanced up. She held back a gasp as she saw Horace being escorted across the balcony by two security guards. Hoping her face had not revealed anything, Estella took her own sip. "I want to be like you," she stated. As she suspected, the Baroness nodded, as if expecting that response. "You're a very powerful woman," said Estella.

"Let me give you some advice," the Baroness said. "If

you have to talk about power, then you don't have it." Her eyes went out over the room and the crowd gathered there for one reason . . . and one reason only–to be near her.

Estella followed her gaze. Despite the hatred she felt toward the woman, Estella had to admit, the Baroness was right. She had infinite power–and wielded it like a weapon.

"Well, I don't have it. Which is why I have to talk about it, which is why I'm here," Estella said. Pandering to the Baroness's ego was the best course of action. "Am I going to have to catch you up a lot, or can you keep up?"

For a moment, the Baroness was silent, and Estella wondered if she had gone too far. Then a smile slowly spread over the woman's face. "You're quite fabulous," she finally said.

Estella exhaled. As she did, she spotted Jasper. He was sneaking out of the servant's entrance dressed in the waiter uniform she had made him. That was good. At least he was safe. Still, they weren't out of the woods yet. She needed more time to finish the job. "So your 1968 collection," she said, lowering her eyes to the lap of her dress. "I loved what you did with embroidery. Talk me through that."

"Where do you come from?" the Baroness said.

Taking a sip of her drink, Estella shrugged. "Up north, sort of. Except a bit south of north. So you'd almost say west." As she gave her vague and ridiculous answer, the Baroness sat back in her seat. The lights from above made the necklace sparkle, and Estella tried to think of a way to get it off the Baroness's neck and into her hands. Up on the balcony, the security guards were looking at something at Horace's feet. Wink, Estella bet. The dog, dressed up as a rat, was probably doing his part. At the same time, she clocked Jasper making his way toward her. She needed to act fast.

But before she could do anything, the Baroness took one last sip of her drink. "I've enjoyed our time together," she said, placing her empty glass on the tray of a passing waiter. "But I guess I'll have you arrested for trespassing now."

Estella's eyes shot up. She hadn't seen that coming. But luckily, she had seen Jasper. He stopped in front of them, holding a tray upon which sat a covered plate. He gave Estella a wink. Then, with a flourish, he pulled the cover off, revealing three beady-eyed rats.

"Is that a rat?" Estella said, jumping to her feet.

The Baroness looked at her and lifted an eyebrow. "Yes," she said, sounding far calmer than she should. "There are three, actually."

As guests nearby took notice and screamed, one of the rats jumped off the tray and into the Baroness's lap. It was just the distraction Estella so desperately needed. As the Baroness tried to free herself from the vermin, Estella slipped behind her and deftly unclasped the necklace. It fell into her hand and then promptly into Buddy's waiting mouth. He took off with it, dodging, unseen, among the feet of the panicked guests.

Not even a moment later, the Baroness's hand went to her neck. Feeling for her jewelry, she let out a cry. "Someone's stolen my necklace!" she shouted.

On the balcony above, Horace took that as his cue. Pulling free of the security guards, he leapt over the railing and dropped down onto the ledge below. Unfortunately, his size wasn't meant for the thin ledge, and he slipped. As he fell, he reached out, grabbing a sash. With a loud rip, he dropped down and swung across the room, slamming into the far wall. The gas pack he had been wearing as part of his "uniform" cracked. Smoke spewed out everywhere, and thrown off-balance, Horace stumbled into the huge cake. Frosting and cake went flying as the table, under the added weight of Horace, broke and crashed to the ground.

The party was in absolute chaos. Standing to the side, the Baroness stared out at the screaming guests. Some ran. Others jumped on any surface they could find and swatted at rats–real and imaginary. Still others just screamed. Taking it all in, the Baroness shook her head. "What," she yelled to no one in particular, "is going on?"

Estella tried not to show the joy she was feeling in the moment. She had done it. They were as good as clear. But as soon as the thought entered her mind, she saw the Baroness's eyes narrow. Following her gaze, Estella saw Buddy, who was racing toward the exit. In his mouth, the necklace glimmered.

"That dog!" the Baroness screamed. "Stop that dog!" Taking a small whistle from a hidden pocket in her gown, she put it to her mouth and blew. A piercing noise filled the air. Instantly, the Dalmatians appeared, their lips pulled back in snarls, their hackles raised.

But it wasn't the sound of the dogs that frightened

Estella. It was the noise. It stabbed at her heart like a knife. She had heard that sound before–the night her mother had fallen. Like a movie she couldn't stop, the scene played out: the Baroness, saying something to her mum and then, a moment later, pulling out the whistle–the very same one–and blowing on it. From behind, Estella had heard the dogs' footsteps and growls. They ran past her, their eyes locked on their owner–whose finger was pointed right at Estella's mum.

Like a bolt of lightning, Estella saw the truth. Her mother hadn't fallen by accident. The Baroness had set her dogs on her. They had driven her over the edge.

The Baroness had killed her mum.

Chapter 14

Barking echoed through the ballroom of the Baroness's mansion. Screams bounced off the walls and pierced the air.

But Estella barely heard it.

Her head and heart were fogged with grief as she stood, the realization of her mum's death pressed upon her.

As Estella tried to steady her racing heart, the sounds of the room returned. She looked around. The place was pandemonium. Nothing elegant remained of the affair. In the chaos, women's hair had come down, men's suit jackets had been ripped. Shreds of black and white littered the floor.

Suddenly, Estella felt someone's hand on her arm. She turned, ready to defend herself, but relaxed when she realized it was just Jasper. With a nod of his head, he gestured for her to follow. The Baroness was no longer paying attention and didn't notice when Estella ran.

Following close behind Jasper, Estella caught sight of Buddy up ahead. In his mouth he still clutched the necklace. Estella cheered him on silently as he got closer and closer to the door. But coming up from behind were the three Dalmatians. Their snarling and snapping became more furious as they got closer to their prey. Estella held back a scream as the second of the three dogs launched onto Buddy.

The small dog vanished under the black-and-white fur. Estella heard a yip and then Buddy reappeared. He still had the necklace. But only for a moment. The big dog reached out and snapped at Buddy, catching the necklace in its mouth. Startled, the Dalmatian swallowed it.

Estella's eyes widened. Jasper and Horace were never going to believe her. To have gone through all that? Only to lose the necklace to a Dalmatian's stomach? It wasn't fair.

Pushed out the front door by the wave of people trying to escape the rat-infested ball, the three friends found themselves looking out at a sea of stalled cars. Drivers were shouting insults at one another as they tried, unsuccessfully, to maneuver away from the mansion. Partygoers popped their heads out the windows, hurling their own insults into the mix. Scanning the packed driveway, Estella spotted their getaway van.

She groaned. It was being towed away.

"Well, here's hoping we've got a plan C," Horace said.

Estella sighed. How had everything gone so terribly wrong? She had planned for every scenario. She had dotted her i's and crossed her t's. And still they were stuck. She shook her head. No. She wasn't failing just because their van got towed. As Horace and Jasper mumbled to each other, Estella slipped down the drive and toward a row of cars whose engines weren't running. Front and center was the Baroness's tan-and-gold DeVille.

Perfect.

Estella opened its door and slid into the front seat.

Making sure no one was watching, she leaned down and quickly pulled the wiring free. In a few swift and practiced moves, she heard the engine roar to life. Smiling, she put it into drive and revved the engine. People dodged out of the way as she sped past, coming to a screeching halt in front of Jasper and Horace.

"Get in!" she yelled.

They didn't hesitate. Jasper flung himself in the front seat as Horace and the two dogs clambered into the back. Then, with a screech of tires and a spray of gravel, Estella peeled out down the driveway.

Estella didn't take her foot off the pedal until the manor was a speck in her rearview mirror and the lights of London flashed in front of her.

Wrenching the wheel to the right, she took a hairpin turn at an alarmingly fast rate. Beside her, Jasper grabbed on to the back of his seat, trying to steady himself. "I didn't know you knew how to drive," he said.

"I don't," Estella answered. Her eyes were full of fury, her knuckles white as she gripped the steering wheel. She knew she probably looked like a madwoman. But she didn't care.

Taking another turn, she vaguely heard Horace and the dogs grunting as they were thrown from one side of the vehicle to the other.

"Estella?" Horace said nervously from the back seat.

She ignored him.

"Estella?" Jasper tried again. "Are you all right?"

She still did not answer. Instead she pushed the pedal down harder, accelerating to an even more dangerous speed. Narrowly missing a pedestrian crossing the street, she yanked the wheel again. Tires screeched and she heard the sound of burning rubber.

"Stop the car!"

Jasper's words startled Estella. As she slammed down on the brakes, the car skidded to a stop. Gasping for breath, Estella fumbled her way out of the car. She felt like the world was closing in on her. She wiped angrily at her eyes as tears fell, unstoppable, down her cheeks. Behind her she heard Jasper and Horace get out of the car. But she didn't turn around. She stared up at the sky, the stars hidden from view by the London smog.

Suddenly, her shoulders sank and she let out a shaky sob. "The Baroness killed my mother," she said. Saying the words out loud gave them weight and made her feel still sicker.

"What are you talking about?" Jasper asked, confused.

"The whistle," Estella said, earning her blank stares from the boys. "She called the dogs on her. It wasn't me. I'd always thought if I had just stayed in the car . . . everything would have been different. If I had been different . . . But she killed her, like she was nothing."

"Cripes," Jasper finally said, finding no other words.

But he didn't need to. Something had shifted in Estella. In saying what had happened out loud, she had taken some of the power and given it back to herself. Her gaze focused. Her shoulders straightened. Then, with a nod, she spun on her heel and got back into the driver's seat. "Let's go," she said to the boys.

Having suffered through the last drive, Jasper and Horace exchanged nervous glances. Then they got in, making sure to buckle their seat belts this time. Before they were even clicked, Estella floored the gas pedal and the car shot off down the dark street.

CHAPTER FOURTEEN

"What are you going to do?" Jasper said when he finally got his breath back and peeled himself away from the seat he had been thrown against.

Estella turned. A cold, wicked smile spread over her face. As they went under a streetlight, her white hair flashed brightly, while her black hair stayed in the shadows. The effect was eerie. "She took everything from me and made me believe I deserved it," Estella said. "And now? My turn."

"What are you talking about?" Jasper asked.

"Revenge," Estella answered simply.

Jasper didn't approve. "You know what they say," he said. "If you're out for revenge you best dig two graves."

Wrenching the wheel, Estella steered the car around a curve. "I thought it was 'revenge is a dish best served cold'?"

"I think that's pork pies," Horace said from the back seat.

Estella glanced at him in the rearview mirror. He was sitting between the two dogs, looking happy as can be. "What?" she said. He was so odd sometimes.

"'Pork pies is a dish best served cold' is the saying," he clarified.

"Point is!" Estella said, her tone sharp. It surprised Jasper and Horace–especially Horace. He was always saying random things and usually Estella didn't care.

She had been trying to keep her cool. But enough was enough. She needed focus. She needed Jasper and Horace to focus.

"Point is," she said again, "the Baroness destroyed my life. So I'm going to return the favor."

Careening by an oncoming car, she laughed darkly. Yes, she was going to return the favor–in spades. The Baroness was going down. And Estella would watch the whole way.

Chapter 15

Estella knew that Jasper and Horace were hoping to lie low for a bit. She had heard them talking from her room when they got back to the Lair. Jasper was especially keen on keeping his head down. To him, the Baroness's party had taken too much energy and too many resources and had been too close.

But Estella didn't want to wait.

She wanted her revenge—now.

The night had been restless. If she closed her eyes,

images of dogs and cliffs and the Baroness's cruel face rushed at her. If she opened them, she was met with a wall of designs and drawings she had done or collected, all in the hopes of garnering favor from the Baroness. By the time the sun peeked over the horizon, Estella had been up for hours. And by the time she heard Jasper and Horace begin their breakfast, she was dressed and primed for action.

Stomping up the stairs to the second level of the loft, Estella burst through a door into the space they had made into their "kitchen". Jasper and Horace sat at a rickety table, eating cereal.

At the sound of her footsteps, they looked up. Both their eyes widened. At nine in the morning, Estella was already decked out in a fancy cocktail dress–black, the lines severe and the fit tight. She looked ready for a fight. As she glanced at the boys, she ran a hand over her black-and-white hair, her kohl-rimmed eyes narrowing.

"Morning, boys," she said in a singsong voice that did not match her attitude or expression. Upon reaching them, she unceremoniously swept their bowls off the table. They clattered to the floor. In their place, she threw down a paper and opened it to the fashion section. The headline jumped out at them. RATS! it read. AND A MYSTERY WOMAN! One large picture showed Estella–the mystery woman–her cloak flaming, while several smaller pictures showed rats racing through the feet of guests.

"So let's begin, shall we?" she said after Jasper and Horace had seen the article.

"You're not going to kill her, are you?" Jasper asked nervously.

Estella shrugged. "It's not part of the current plan," she answered. "But we might have to be adaptable."

"So that's a no?" Jasper said hopefully. But his face had grown pale.

"If you heard a no, it is," Estella said vaguely. This only caused Jasper's face to become more ghostly. "Now, the necklace. One of the Dalmatians ate it. Not sure which one. So you'll have to kidnap all of them."

Jasper's mouth dropped open. "Wait, what?"

Estella rolled her eyes. He was being so dense. It wasn't like this was the first time they had done something illegal. If this was going to work, he needed to stop being so . . . moral. "Darling," she said, adopting the new, posh accent she had used the night before, "if I'm going to have to repeat myself, this isn't going to work out." Ignoring

Jasper's confused look, Estella went on. "The necklace went in one end. It's going to come out the other. That's how it works." Her first order of the day given, she turned toward the old, derelict elevator they used to get up and down.

Behind her, she heard Horace mumble about his breakfast. At least he wasn't pushing back. But Jasper was. "What's the rest of the plan?" he called after her. "And where are you going?"

Estella didn't even bother to turn around. She waved off his worries. "Need-to-know basis," she said. Then, without another word, she stepped inside the elevator. As the doors closed, she heard Jasper sigh.

"That's not how we usually work," he said.

He was right. But nothing was usual anymore. Everything had changed.

All the way to the *Tattletale* office, Estella thought about her interactions with Jasper and Horace. She felt bad. Sort of. But they had to understand what she was going through. The bandage over her mum's death had been ripped off painfully, and it felt as though her heart were bleeding. True, she shouldn't have knocked Horace's cereal to the floor. And she probably shouldn't have copped an attitude–or accent–with Jasper. But in both cases, it was an issue of survival.

Survival and revenge.

Those thoughts were still on her mind as she came to a stop in front of the *Tattletale* office. Craning her neck up, she took in the stone facade and imposing gold signage. It was bold and a bit trashy–which summed up the paper nicely. Pushing open the doors, she strutted into the lobby.

She didn't have to wait long once she gave her name at the front desk. Moments later, she heard the click-clack of Anita Darling's heels as the young woman made her way over. Stopping in front of Estella, Anita smiled hesitantly.

"Anita Darling, my darling!" Estella said, leaning down and air-kissing the journalist's cheeks. Then Anita gestured toward the elevators. Together, the women entered and made their way up to Anita's desk. When they were seated, Anita sat back and raised an eyebrow.

Estella lifted her own. She had recognized Anita almost immediately at the party. You could dress a girl up and take her out of the country, Estella thought, but you couldn't take the country out of her. Anita was the same girl she had met on her first day at school. The only one who had been nice to her—at least at the beginning.

"Estella!" Anita began, making it clear she had made the connection, too. "It's been so long. It's so good to see you. I kept staring at you at the party. And then it came to me. That's Estella."

Nodding, Estella crossed her long legs. "So, you go to parties, take pictures, print gossip," she said. "That's your job?"

Anita shrugged, looking embarrassed. "It's not as fun as it sounds."

Truth be told, Estella didn't care if Anita liked her job or not. That wasn't why she had walked all the way to *Tattletale* or taken the chance of reconnecting with an old "friend". "It sounds useful," she corrected.

Anita cocked her head, curious.

Good, Estella thought, seeing the look. She needed Anita to be curious. "I'd like to start my own label," Estella began. "Why don't we work together and create some buzz for this old rag you continually fill with that old hag?"

For a moment, Anita was silent, staring across the desk

at Estella with an unreadable expression. "You have that glint in your eye," Anita finally said.

"What glint?"

"I'm starting to remember you have an extreme side," Anita said.

Estella smiled. Some might call it extreme; she called it survival. "Then you also remember what fun that is," she said. Getting to her feet, she leaned over, her fingers splayed out over the latest edition of *Tattletale*. Intentionally, she made sure she blocked the images of the Baroness that littered the page. "Now, I want you to help me tell them who I am."

The women's eyes met. Then, together, they smiled.

Estella was pleased. She had a deal with Anita. She had made headlines already with last night's "show". Now she just needed to build upon the momentum–and hope that Jasper and Horace were doing their job.

At that very moment, Jasper and Horace were sitting in a van, staring across the street at one of the poshest dog groomers in London. Estella had made it clear: they were to stay where they were until they spotted the Baroness's Dalmatians; then they were to steal them. "It shouldn't be hard," she'd instructed earlier, her voice sounding more Cruella than Estella. Jasper didn't like it. He didn't like much of anything that had been happening lately. It all seemed out of control, and Estella's demands and expectations were becoming more unrealistic. He felt like his friend was slipping away, growing more comfortable in her role as Cruella. On the plus side, the downtime was kind of nice. He and Horace had spent most of the morning just listening to a football match on the radio.

Noticing a small woman carrying a pocket-size pup into the groomers, Horace cocked his head. "You ever notice how some dog owners look a lot like their dogs?" he asked Jasper. As he spoke, Horace looked down at Wink, who looked back at him with an eerily similar expression.

Jasper suppressed a smile. "No," he said, trying not to laugh as Horace and Wink sneezed at the same time. "I've never noticed that." Horace could be a goof, but Jasper loved him like a brother. As he watched, Horace put one hand over his eye and looked back at a new dog and owner as they sauntered past as if that might give him a new perspective.

CHAPTER FIFTEEN

Shaking his head, Jasper took a deep breath. It was time to get down to business. If they didn't return to the Lair with the Dalmatians–and the necklace that was sitting in one of their stomachs–Estella would be furious. And he didn't want to deal with her fury–again. "Let's have a bit of focus. We've got a job to do."

Horace looked down at Wink again. The dog was a key part of the plan they had worked out to get the Dalmatians out of the salon and into the van. "Wink is a very likable dog," Horace said. "I'm not sure it'll work."

"It'll work," Jasper said. He was banking on the Dalmatians' remembering Wink from the party–or at least recognizing his smell.

Getting out of the van, Jasper grabbed Wink and headed across the street, while Horace moved to the back and opened the doors. Through the windows of the groomers, Jasper saw the Dalmatians in varying stages of pampering, from being covered in bubbles to having their coats dried and nails trimmed. They were all facing the door. Jasper nodded. That was good.

As he pushed open the door, the dogs lifted their heads. Wink stood, trembling, in the doorway for only a moment. But that was all it took. The dogs growled, and then they began to bark. Then they all leapt off their tables and gave chase. Wink turned and hightailed it back across the street as the Dalmatians followed. Horace was in position, and as Wink leapt into his arms, the Dalmatians' momentum carried them into the back of the van. Horace slammed the door shut, trapping them inside.

Moments later, Jasper and Horace were back in their seats. Gunning the engine, Jasper steered the van into the busy streets of London. Before the groomers could even figure out what had happened, the van–carrying its precious cargo–had disappeared from sight.

Jasper turned and gave Horace a smile. "You don't have to say I was right," he said.

Horace shook his head. He just didn't get it. How could anyone–or any dog–want to hurt Wink?

Turning a corner, Jasper settled back in his seat. They had the dogs. Now they just had to sit and wait until one of them "produced" the necklace.

Estella looked down at her watch. If Jasper and Horace were on schedule, right about now they would be using Wink to lure the Dalmatians out of the doggy spa and into a waiting van. There was no way for her to know if they were successful until she got back to the Lair later. But for now she was going to assume that the boys had it under control.

Focusing, she made her way toward her next stop: Artie's vintage clothing shop.

She didn't pay attention to the stares of passersby as she made her way down the busy London streets. She knew that she cut quite the picture–tight black dress, black-and-white hair, serious expression. But for once she wasn't trying to hide. Let them look. Let them gawk. She had spent far too long hiding behind fake hair and living a lie. She was ready for the world to know Cruella.

Pushing open the door of Artie's shop, she heard the familiar chime of the bell. Artie looked up from his copy of *Tattletale*. Seeing her, his eyes dropped back to the page and then lifted back to her. "It's you," he said, awe in his voice.

Estella nodded. "It is," she replied.

"And you're in my shop," he said.

"I've been here before," she pointed out as she walked closer. He looked at her, confused. "I got my dress here. It's me, Estella."

Realization came over his face. Hurrying around from

behind the counter, he took in her outfit. The dress. The hair. The makeup. Then he nodded, impressed. "You certainly made a stir. Well done."

Estella smiled. Artie's reaction was just what she had hoped it would be. Like Anita, he was vital to her plan. She had figured Anita would be hungry enough to help her, but she hadn't been as sure about Artie. From the looks of it, though, he was hungry, too. She went on. "I need some help. I want to make art, Artie, and I want to make trouble. You in?"

The young man didn't hesitate. "I'm in," he said, grabbing his coat. "I do so love trouble."

The words were music to her ears. Grabbing a few items off the nearest rack, Estella quickly gave Artie a list of what else she needed. As he grabbed his sewing machine and a few more dresses, Estella allowed herself to take a breath. She had been going full tilt since the night before. She wanted to take a moment to relax. But she knew that now was not the time. Satisfied that they had everything they needed, Estella turned and headed out of the store. Artie followed. She was one step closer to getting her revenge. And she couldn't wait to serve it–hot or cold.

Chapter 16

Estella sailed into the Lair. Artie was close behind, his steps a bit slower under the weight of his sewing machine and the extra clothes. Scanning the space, Estella saw one Dalmatian tearing up a set of old books, while another lunged toward them, knocking over a lamp in the process. The third had Horace backed into a corner.

"Ah, you got them," she said. Horace nodded nervously.

Coming around the corner, Jasper's steps slowed as he saw Estella—and Artie.

"Artie–boys. Boys–Artie," she said with a wave of her hand.

The Dalmatian in front of Horace barked loudly, causing Horace to shake. "They're very aggressive," he said. On cue, the other dogs joined in the barking, making the whole room sound like a kennel.

Estella shrugged. "You need to walk them. Feed them," she stated, ignoring the fear in Horace's face. "We need to get that necklace out."

Jasper shot her a look. "You're welcome," he said, a hint of bitterness in his voice. "You could help."

Horace nodded in agreement. "Why can't you walk them as well?" he said. "There's no 'I' in team."

"There is an 'I' in imbecile," Estella snapped. "Go!" She didn't have time for this. She needed the boys working on the dogs while she handled other things. How did they not get that? Did they not know how much this all meant to her?

Apparently not. Jasper shook his head. "You can't talk to us like that," he said, his voice raised. "We're helping you."

"So don't."

CHAPTER SIXTEEN

The room became silent. Even the dogs stopped barking. Estella stared at Jasper, not breaking her gaze. She was done playing nice. If dealing with the Baroness had taught her anything, it was to look after priority number one–herself.

Artie's head snapped back and forth between Estella and Jasper. Finally, after hefting the sewing machine on his hip, he headed toward the stairs. "Mum and Dad are fighting," he said, clearly trying to bring some levity to the situation. "I'll set up downstairs."

As Artie left and Horace headed outside with the dogs, Estella's eyes didn't leave Jasper. They had never had a real fight before, and it made her feel bad–but also annoyed. Jasper had always had her back. And now he just seemed to be standing in her way. Didn't he understand what all of this meant to her? It wasn't just about bringing the Baroness down. Well, maybe it was a *lot* about that. But there was more. Her designs were being noticed. Her fashion was being talked about. The dream Estella had not dared dream–having a label of her own–seemed close. And she didn't want to lose that–not when she had lost so much already.

"You could be more polite," Jasper finally said.

"I don't have time," she said, brushing off his comment. "I have to go to work. I'm a designer now."

Now Jasper looked surprised. "Seriously?"

She nodded. "Keep your enemies close," she said. She turned and walked to a large bin of random costumes and wigs. She dug through it until she found what she was looking for. Standing up, she brandished a red wig in the air. "Voila!" she said happily. "Cruella was in a box for a long time. Now Estella can be the one who makes guest appearances."

It was easier to "play" Estella than Estella had thought it would be. With the red wig on her head and glasses on her nose, no one even took notice of her as she walked into the Baroness's warehouse.

No one that is, except Jeffrey. Spotting her, he gestured to her frantically.

"She wants you," he said when she stopped in front of him. "Hurry!"

Estella made her way to the office, but she paused just

outside the doors. Through the door she saw the Baroness, her face red with rage. John stood to one side, his own face, as usual, unreadable. The Baroness yelled and threw a copy of *Tattletale* to the ground. It landed among a pile of other papers. Staring back at Estella from their pages were images of the Baroness, partygoers gone crazy, and Cruella.

"Everyone's laughing at me," the Baroness said, pointing at the papers.

John shook his head, trying to soothe the savage Baroness. "All press is good press, Baroness," he tried, earning him a sharp look. He backpedaled. "Although they have rather focused on the rats . . ."

The Baroness didn't acknowledge the vermin. Instead, she asked, "Did you happen to notice her hair?"

Outside the office, Estella was puzzled by what she had overheard. Why did the Baroness care about Cruella's hair? The valet waved away the woman's concern. "Coincidence," he said. "Apparently the young people are all doing it nowadays."

Are they? Estella thought. That seemed a bit of a stretch, even for John.

"Are they?" the Baroness said, echoing Estella's thought. Like her, she did not sound convinced.

John nodded. As he started to give her justifications, Estella took a deep breath. She wasn't going to just stand there. As she pushed her way into the room, the Baroness looked up, startled to be interrupted. Seeing that it was just Estella, the Baroness frowned. "Ah, here she is," she said. "Late, but clearly happy to have her wages docked thirty percent."

Estella didn't get the opportunity to respond as the Baroness plunged ahead. "Grab a pad," she ordered, gesturing to a stack on her desk. Picking one up, Estella snagged a pencil and waited.

The Baroness strode to the far side of the office and walked out onto the balcony. She glared down at the workroom below, banging her hand on the railing. Everyone on the floor looked up. Immediately, the room grew silent.

"My spring collection," she stated. "I need twelve pieces and I have . . . let me count." She paused, and moved to a large board with half a dozen designs pinned to it. One by one she ripped them off and crumpled them into balls. Behind her, Estella winced. That was months of work from the designers, destroyed. "Zero! Go! I want ten pieces that work by three a.m.!" she screamed, turning back to Estella.

"Thank you," Estella said.

"Gratitude is for losers," the Baroness snapped. Her tone was sharp and cold.

Estella couldn't help noticing how differently she had spoken to Cruella. There had been a level of respect to their conversation. But not for Estella. The simmering anger in her heart heated up. She tamped it down slightly. But she prodded the beast a little bit more. "Good advice," she said. Then, very intentionally, she added, "Thanks."

"What did I just say?"

"Don't say 'thank you,'" she said, holding back the feeling of joy she got from goading the Baroness. "Got it. Thank you." The "accidental" slip of the tongue earned her another glare from the Baroness. Luckily, at that moment, the phone on the desk rang loudly.

Storming over, the Baroness ripped it off the cradle. Her furious expression became still more furious as the voice on the other end of the line mumbled something. "What do you mean the dogs are gone?" she screamed when the other voice stopped. "Find them!"

That was Estella's cue. Slipping out the door, she

suppressed a smile. She was glad that she had been there when the call came in. Seeing the Baroness's angry expression almost made up for the verbal lashing she had received. Almost.

But it didn't matter what the Baroness said or did to Estella. Because, Estella thought as she entered the work-room, Cruella was going to have the last laugh–starting that night, when she made another "guest appearance" at one of the Baroness's events.

Chapter 17

Estella had been cutting it close. She couldn't duck out of the workroom before the Baroness left for the day or that would draw attention to her. But the Baroness had taken an exasperatingly long time trying to pick out an outfit to wear to the evening's soiree—a red-carpet premiere. By the time she finally settled on a dress and had slipped inside the limo, Estella had not even an hour to get back to the Lair, change from Estella to Cruella, and get to the premiere.

Tucked out of sight in an alley, Estella watched as the long line of limos approached the red carpet, slowed to a stop, and let out their occupants. Cameras flashed, reporters called out questions, and, depending on the star, screams grew louder. The air was full of excitement, and the guest list was a who's who of the entertainment and fashion world. Estella saw two rock stars, no fewer than five A-list movie stars, and half a dozen directors–and that was in just the four minutes she had been standing in the alley.

When she made her move, it was going to be epic.

Scanning down the row of limos, she spotted the Baroness's car. Good. She had made it in time. She squinted at the crowd of people who had gathered behind the heavy velvet ropes used to separate the stars from the hoi polloi. She nodded again. Jasper and Horace were in position. Catching her eye, Jasper tilted his hat toward her. She held up a finger. *Wait,* she mouthed.

Confident that Jasper and Horace were ready, Estella took a minute to put the finishing touches on her own outfit. Pulling a can of spray paint out of her bag, she got to work. Her hand flew, paint spraying. When she was done, she looked down at her masterpiece. *Perfect,* she thought with a smile.

Glancing once more out of the alley, she saw that the Baroness's car had moved forward. She was one car away from the entrance. Jasper and Horace slipped under the velvet ropes. As the Baroness's car came to a stop in front of the red carpet, they positioned themselves on either side of it and threaded a huge leather strap under and over the car, directly in front of the Baroness's door. She was trapped inside.

Estella took a deep breath. Then she sprinted across the street toward the car. Inside, the Baroness pounded and screamed. Outside, Estella leapt onto the roof of the car. Instantly, dozens of cameras turned in her direction. As the bulbs began to flash, Estella twirled. Faster and faster she spun, her fluorescent pink gown floating up and out until she was just a blur of pink. She heard the paparazzi calling out for her name, for the designer of the dress, but Estella kept spinning. As she did, her skirt unraveled, layer by layer. With each layer, a jagged piece of spray paint art was revealed.

Beneath her, Estella heard the Baroness's angry

screams. She knew she had to wrap it up. If she was going to build a mystery, she couldn't very well get caught. With one final spin, the last of her skirt came free from its place around her waist and fell down over the car. As she sprinted off, her neon pink pants sparkling, she heard gasps from the crowd.

Turning, she took a quick moment to appreciate her handiwork. The Baroness's car was now covered by the pink skirt. And written in bold, messy red spray paint that made the whole thing look like a modern work of art were the words *the past*.

Estella caught a glimpse of the Baroness's face inside the car. It was pressed up against the window as the woman desperately tried to see what was happening.

Estella laughed. She had done it. She had made a fool of the Baroness. She was one step closer to having her revenge and putting her past in the past.

The Baroness was furious. She had been humiliated and was now taking it out on her staff. Head bent over the morning's paper—complete with a big picture of her dress-covered car—she stalked back and forth in front of the designers who all stood, shaking in their stiff shoes. At the end of the line, Estella stood, feeling slightly guilty. This was, in part, her fault—or at least Cruella's.

Her stunt at the premiere had paid off. Everyone who was anyone—and a lot of people who were not—was talking about it and wondering about the real identity of the mysterious black-and-white-haired fashionista who went by Cruella. Most people were intrigued. The Baroness was just angry.

"We have no signature piece," the Baroness said, stomping up to the nine design sketches pinned to a corkboard. In the middle was a large space where a design should be. "And this Cruella person is everywhere! I want ideas!"

Throwing the paper at Jeffrey, the Baroness turned and looked at Estella. Estella swallowed nervously. She didn't like the look in the Baroness's eyes.

"Estella," she said, walking over and grabbing the sketch pad from her hands, "You're my last hope. What have you got?" She flipped through the designs, pausing on some, scowling at others, frowning at still more.

Estella watched. "You seem upset," she said.

The Baroness's head snapped up. "My dogs have gone missing, my necklace has been stolen, and this Cruella creature is . . ." Her voice trailed off and Estella felt herself leaning forward, curious to hear what the Baroness would say. But instead of finishing that thought, the Baroness shook her head. "This show has to be the best!" she said instead.

Playing the part of helpful assistant, Estella nodded sympathetically. "Now you seem unhinged," she said, trying not to sound as happy about that as she was. "Can I get you some cucumber? Thinly sliced?"

"Go!" the Baroness shouted, throwing Estella's sketch pad at her while she screamed. "Go and get your desiccated, dried-out brain working!"

"Of course," Estella said, biting back what she really wanted to say about who was dried up and desiccated.

Turning to the rest of the designers, the Baroness swung an arm out toward the workstations. "The rest of you," she snapped, "get back to work." Without another word, she turned and stalked out of the workroom and up the stairs to her office. A moment later, the door slammed.

Estella knew that what she should do was work on designs for the Baroness. But after the last few days, she was inspired to do more than that. And a lunch break was technically a "break", so while she was eating, she might as well use the time to her own advantage. Grabbing her bagged lunch and her own sketch pad, Estella slipped away from her desk.

She quickly made her way down the winding halls that were now as familiar to her as the Lair. She had spent so many hours in this building. Sweating and worrying, all for a woman who didn't deserve her talents or time. If she could, Estella would give up everything to have her mother back. But since that was not possible, she was going to settle for the next best thing–making sure her mum hadn't died in vain. The House of Baroness would not be the end of Estella's passion for design. She wouldn't give the Baroness the satisfaction of taking everything. She would use what she had learned and the doors the Baroness had unwittingly opened to become a fashion designer the likes of which London–and even the world–hadn't seen.

But first she needed to finish dealing with the Baroness.

Coming to the end of one long hall, Estella pushed open the emergency door. She knew the alarm wouldn't sound. The delivery guys used the entrance to sneak out and take a break when they could. The alley behind was private and quiet. It was a perfect spot for Estella to get some work done.

She settled herself up against a corner of the alley. Taking an apple out of her lunch bag, she crunched down, waiting for inspiration to strike. It didn't take long. Within a few moments her hand was racing across the page as a dress came to life on the paper. Her head bent over, she didn't notice the door to the alley open and two huge security guards appear. Only when their shadows fell over the dress did she look up.

Her eyes widened.

One of the security guards reached out with a huge meaty hand and grabbed the sketch pad from Estella. The other one grabbed her and hauled her to her feet. Not saying a word, they led her back into the warehouse–and straight toward the Baroness's office.

"That's mine!" Estella cried helplessly as they went further into the warehouse. The men ignored her. She struggled against the security guard's grip, but it was useless. Panic and fear flooded through her. If the Baroness saw that sketch . . . She shuddered. It could blow her cover and ruin her plans of revenge before they could even get started. How had the woman even known to look for her in the alley? Then it came to her. Cameras. The woman was so paranoid. Of course she had cameras everywhere.

Before she could think any more about what a breach of trust that was, they arrived at the Baroness's office. The two guards shoved her inside and then dropped her sketch pad on the desk in front of the Baroness.

Casually, as if people were dragged in front of her every day, the Baroness leaned against her desk. She picked up the pad and rifled through it, stopping at the latest sketch. Her eyes scanned the page, her face emotionless except for the slightest twitch of her lip.

She had been right. That was no surprise; she was usually right. But she found herself oddly bothered by it now. Estella's behavior had seemed off. And in the Baroness's world, when someone seemed off, it was usually because they were trying to stab her in the back. So she had had the cameras follow Estella when she left on her lunch break and then watched as the girl designed the fantastic dress she now held in her hand.

"Estella," the Baroness finally said, drawing out the girl's name. "I'm surprised by you. Holding out on me."

"But I was on lunch break," Estella protested weakly. "In a public space," she added.

"I own the alley," the Baroness replied haughtily.

Estella's eyebrows shot up. "Really?" she said. "You can own alleys?"

The Baroness nodded as if that were the most obvious thing in the world. "Alleys, designs, people," she said, then paused before she added, "their souls." As if to emphasize her point, the Baroness ripped the sketch clean out of Estella's pad. "Check your employment contract."

The Baroness stalked over to the large design board that dominated the far wall, and pinned the sketch in the middle. Taking a step back, she crossed her arms over her chest and cocked her head. "I think I just found my signature piece," she said. "What do you think?" Turning, she shot Estella a glare, daring her to respond.

The Baroness watched the range of emotions fly across Estella's face. She knew what the girl was thinking. She was thinking she wanted to tell the Baroness exactly what she thought about her idea and where she could shove it. But she was also thinking that if she did that, she would lose her job. And this job was everything to the ragamuffin. Given the clothes she wore and her terrible dye job, it was clear Estella needed the money. So she could think whatever she wanted. It wasn't going to change the fact that the Baroness was going to use her design—as her own.

Waving a hand, she dismissed Estella and picked up the phone. She wouldn't fire her yet. Taking the dress would be her punishment, and hopefully she would learn her lesson. You don't go up against the Baroness—ever.

Fuming, Estella walked to the door. The Baroness was a monster—a horrible monster who relished destroying others. But not for long. Estella—or Cruella—was going to take her down a peg or two. Let her think she had the upper hand. She'd find out soon enough how wrong she was, and right now Estella just wanted to get out of the office with the rest of her sketch pad intact. If the Baroness had looked past the newest design, she might have noticed some familiar gowns—like the Black and White Ball gown or the pink one from the previous night. It had been too close for comfort.

Estella stopped in the doorway. Framed by the door, her face was cast in shadow as she spoke. "Can I do anything else for you today, Baroness?" she asked, hoping that the shadows would hide the anger in her eyes.

Still on the phone, the Baroness waved her off, not even meeting her gaze. Just like that, she was dismissed for the day.

That was perfectly fine with Estella. She had to get back to the Lair. The Baroness was attending an event that evening, and after the day Estella had had, she was in the mood to let Cruella loose to wreak a little fashion havoc.

Chapter 18

The Baroness was growing tired of Cruella.

The mysterious woman had ruined another event. As the Baroness stood on another red carpet, posing for the paparazzi and ignoring the rest of the crowd, a large garbage truck had appeared. Emblazoned on its side was the Baroness's logo. The Baroness had watched, momentarily struck speechless, as the garbage truck backed up toward the carpet. The huge back lifted up and then tilted down, spilling dozens of dresses–the Baroness's dresses–onto the ground like, well, garbage.

As the paparazzi turned to start shooting the garbage rather than the Baroness, the dresses began to move. A moment later, Cruella emerged from the pile of clothes. In a stunning gown, presumably of her own design, she lifted her arms and waved at the crowd. A spotlight appeared from somewhere, shining on her and making her look like a trophy on top of a pile of trash. Cruella jumped up onto the garbage truck, then gave one last wave as it moved down the street, pulling the dresses behind it like the train of a gown.

The Baroness had watched, fuming. Why did Cruella keep stealing her spotlight?

She was still stewing the next morning when her two most trusted bodyguards appeared in her office. Looking up from the pile of papers, she shot the men looks. She pointed to the papers. All of them had pictures of Cruella plastered on the front.

"Have you found her?" she asked.

The two men shook their heads.

"She's a ghost," one of them said.

This was not the answer the Baroness wanted. She was about to turn her fury on the men when the door to her office opened again. Roger stumbled in. The lawyer looked tired, his clothes rumpled and his hair a mess. He had, per the Baroness's orders, been up all night trying to find out about the mysterious Cruella.

"Anything?" the Baroness asked. She didn't care that he was tired. It was his job to be tired so she wouldn't have to be.

Like the guards, he shook his head. "I couldn't find anything on her," he said nervously.

Anger flooded through the Baroness. Was everyone around her completely incompetent? Ordering the two security guards out, she turned to do the same to Roger. But as she did, her eyes landed on the byline for *Tattletale*'s most recent Cruella article. Anita Darling's name jumped out at her.

The Baroness paused, considering. She'd always said that if you wanted to get something done right, do it yourself. Standing up, she gestured for Roger to follow her. She was going to make a little trip to see Anita Darling. Maybe then she would get some answers.

Anita Darling was tired. But happy. All the Cruella coverage had given her an in with her boss, and she was getting more and more assignments. Leaning over a small mirror on her desk, she applied another coat of mascara. She was supposed to be heading downtown for an event and was already late.

Hearing footsteps, she looked up and gulped. It was the Baroness.

Sweeping into the *Tattletale* offices, she made her way to Anita's desk. Behind her were the two big goons who served as her bodyguards. When she got to Anita's desk, the Baroness unceremoniously threw a copy of *Tattletale* down. Then she stood back, arms crossed.

"You'll need more than eyeliner, you plain little thing," the Baroness said, no trace of humor in her voice. "You do, however, have an eye for a good shot." She nodded at the picture of Cruella staring up at both of them.

Anita took a breath and tried to calm her racing heart. "Baroness," she said, hoping her voice sounded even.

The woman ignored her and went on. "I suddenly realized in all the coverage of Cruella, you always have the best shot. The best angle." She paused and leaned closer. "Like you're ready for it . . ."

Anita gulped. "Just lucky, I guess."

The Baroness shook her head. She wasn't buying it. "It's like you know," she went on. "Like you're a part of it." Her eyes narrowed and her lips curled back. Anita couldn't help thinking the woman resembled a snake about to strike as she hissed, "Who is she? And more importantly, where is she?"

"I don't know," Anita said, trying her best to sound convincing. She couldn't let Estella down. But the Baroness's eyes drilled into her, making her blood run cold and her cheeks grow hot. Under the woman's gaze, she felt her strength fading.

"Did you just *lie* to me?" the Baroness snarled.

The Baroness was a force. She could ruin Anita's career—her life. "I . . . I . . ." she stammered, trying to think of something, anything, to say to get out of the situation.

"Don't cry," the Baroness said.

Anita cocked her head, confused. "I'm not," she said.

Turning to go, the Baroness sighed. "You will," she said, her meaning clear. If Anita didn't fess up and help her, she would regret it. Watching as the woman sauntered toward the elevators, Anita let out her breath in a whoosh. She had managed to keep Estella's identity secret–for now. But she wasn't sure how long she could protect her friend. When the Baroness wanted something, she got it . . . whatever, or whomever, the cost.

Sliding into the back of her car, the Baroness snarled at Roger. Per her orders, the lawyer had waited for her while she talked to Anita. He looked up from his papers and paled at the fury on the Baroness's face.

"We need to sue her," she growled. She began to rattle off a list of possible offenses Anita had committed. "Defamation. False imprisonment. Vandalism. Something!"

Roger shifted uncomfortably in his seat. The Baroness's anger filled the space, and he felt the blood drain from his face. The Baroness stared at him, waiting. "Well, we haven't really, um . . ." he started. The Baroness gave him a blank look, and he rushed ahead. "Having been through the statutes and talked to the police, I'm not sure what our legal avenues are–"

The Baroness cut him off. "I need you to stop talking, Roger."

He looked surprised. "You do?"

She nodded. She had asked him to do one thing–find a way to rid her of the nuisance known as Cruella. He had failed. And the Baroness did not tolerate failure. "You're fired," she said simply. Roger's face fell, but the Baroness felt nothing. He was nothing to her. He could go play a sad song on his little piano for pennies for all she cared. Gesturing to the door, she made it clear he needed to go.

Roger fumbled with the handle, his hand shaking. The door wouldn't open. "Sorry," he said. "But how do you open this door?"

The Baroness suppressed a groan. Could the man do nothing? Wrenching the handle one more time, Roger finally swung the door open and slipped out of the car. Turning, he started to say something, but the Baroness stopped him with a stare. She had things to do and people to see–and Roger was no longer one of those people.

Slamming the door in his face, she signaled to the driver to go. She had to get back to the warehouse and fix things before they got even more out of control.

Chapter 19

Estella stood by her work space in the warehouse. Her eyes were glued to the board across the room. Pinned smack in the center was her sketch. She had never intended for that design to be seen by the Baroness. It was one of her own—or one of Cruella's. She sometimes couldn't tell who she was when she was in the middle of a design. Either way, when the Baroness had ripped it from the sketchbook, she had claimed it as her own. Estella wasn't sure what irked her more—the fact that the Baroness technically had the right to do that, or the fact that Estella had been foolish enough to put the sketch in such a vulnerable spot in the first place.

Hearing angry footsteps, Estella turned to see the Baroness storming into the designers' area. Estella immediately pretended to look intently at the piece of fabric in her hand.

"Where's the beading for the dress?" the Baroness barked as she strode past Estella.

"Ordered," Estella said. "Just waiting on this idiot deliveryman." As the words slipped from her mouth, Estella repressed a gasp. She had accidently said them in her Cruella voice. The Baroness's steps slowed.

Nervously, Estella held her breath, waiting to see if the Baroness had noticed. The woman gave her a look, but then, with a shrug, she moved on. Estella let out her breath again. That had been too close. She had to be more careful. One more slip and she could give her identity away and end up ruining her own future rather than the Baroness's.

She spotted Horace, dressed in a deliveryman's uniform, wheeling a cart toward her. A box was placed on top. Seeing him, Estella smiled.

"Top of the morning, missy," Horace said, greeting her with a ridiculous accent. He nodded at the box. "Got some fashion items most fashionable."

"Thank you, handsome deliveryman," she said, earning her a grin from Horace. She had never in her life called him handsome.

Glancing around to be sure no one was listening, Horace leaned in. "How you doin'?"

"Don't break character," she hissed back. Estella knew she had reacted harshly, but he had to know what was at stake. They were in the serpent's lair. At any moment, the Baroness could appear.

He took a step back, surprised by the venom in her tone. "Me break character?" he said. "You called me handsome." Shrugging, he raised his voice back to a normal conversational tone and pointed to the box. "All right, missy. There we are–have a look." Peeling back the box's top with a crowbar, he revealed the contents.

Inside, dozens upon dozens of beautiful iridescent beads gleamed and sparkled. Estella sucked in a breath. They were the most beautiful things she had ever seen. Better than she had imagined when she ordered them.

They would make any gown shine–and a gown of her design? It would be one of a kind. Lifting her eyes, Estella saw that Horace was also gobsmacked by their beauty. She smiled, her fingers itching to touch them. But sensing someone's eyes on her, she looked up. She saw from inside her office the Baroness staring down at her, her eyes cold and calculating.

Estella gulped.

Waving Horace off, she turned her attention to the beads. It was time to get to work. Pulling a mannequin over to her space, Estella sat down and started to sew. Soon she was lost in the rhythm of her creativity. The sound of the sewing machines faded away. The chatter became white noise. She didn't notice as, one by one, the other designers packed up their things and headed home for the night. Piece by piece, Estella stitched and sewed, weaving bead after iridescent bead onto the emerging gown.

The sun sank and the stars came out, and still Estella worked. She ignored the late-night cleaning crew, lifting her feet as they swept up the discarded pieces of fabric beneath her. She didn't even acknowledge her own rumbling stomach or the ache growing between her shoulder blades as she hunched over. She was overcome by the design. She was making something brilliant; something beautiful; something unique.

Finally, as the first birds chirped their morning song, Estella sat back. Stretching her arms high over her head, she stared at the gown in front of her. It was the most amazing thing she had ever created. The lines were tight. The stitching invisible. It glimmered and shone under the warehouse lights, almost appearing to come alive. Estella smiled, awash with pride.

And now she was going to have to give it to the Baroness.

By the time the Baroness and the rest of the design team finally arrived, Estella was nearly asleep on her feet, the late night catching up to her. But upon hearing the Baroness's voice, she snapped to attention.

Striding into the designers' space, the Baroness made her way to Estella and the gown. She did not speak as she walked around the mannequin. Behind her, Estella saw the other designers come in. Spotting the Baroness and the dress, they began to whisper to each other in awe.

Finally, the Baroness stopped her inspection. "Well, I've

done it again," she said, giving Estella a look that dared her to defy the statement. "Let's go make history. My best show ever. Estella," she added, gesturing to her. "Come with me. I need a drink."

You *do?* Estella thought bitterly. I'm *the one who did all this.* But she kept her thoughts to herself and instead, with one last look at her gown, followed the woman out to her car.

Estella and the Baroness sat in a booth in the back corner of one of London's swankiest restaurants. In front of them, a nervous waiter fumbled with the champagne bottle. Under the Baroness's cold gaze, the waiter's hands shook as he tried to pull the cork, but it would not budge. Growing impatient, the Baroness leaned over and grabbed the bottle. "Give it to me," she snapped. Then, in one smooth, well-practiced move, she popped the cork–sending the top flying right into the back of the retreating waiter. The Baroness didn't skip a beat. Pouring herself a glass, she offered one to Estella.

"Here's to me," she said, raising the glass.

Estella couldn't help it. She laughed.

The Baroness shot her a look. "Who else would I drink too?" she asked.

"Me?" Estella suggested boldly. "For doing the signature piece."

The Baroness waved the suggestion off. "You're helpful to me, that's all," she said. "As soon as you're not, you're dust."

"Inspiring talk. Thank you." Estella couldn't help herself. The woman was incorrigible.

The sarcasm, however, was lost on the Baroness. "You can't care about anyone else, because everyone is an obstacle," she said. She took a sip of her champagne and went on. "You care about what that obstacle feels or wants, you're dead. If I had cared about anyone or -thing, I might have died, like so many brilliant women, with a drawer full of unseen genius and a heart full of sad bitterness." Estella was surprised. The Baroness actually sounded–human. Her next words surprised her even more. "You have the talent for your own label. Whether you have a killer instinct is the big question."

We both know you *do,* Estella thought, visualizing her mother. But aloud, she simply spoke the truth: "I hope I do."

The Baroness nodded quickly. "Correct response. Well done," she said. "We just need to lose this Cruella person. Don't you think?"

"I guess you must hate her," Estella said, hoping her face hadn't flushed at the mention of her alter ego.

"Honestly? I'm conflicted," the Baroness answered after a moment. "She is good. Bold and brilliant. But she's made it me or her, so I'm going to have to destroy her." Lifting her glass to her lips, the Baroness leveled her gaze at Estella.

Estella shifted in her seat nervously. There was a look in the Baroness's eyes she didn't like.

"Cheers," the Baroness said.

Clinking her glass against the older woman's, Estella cheered her back. Her hand was steady, but inside, she was shaking. Could the Baroness know who she really was? And if she did, what would she do with that knowledge?

Chapter 20

For once Jasper was happy about the clouds that constantly seemed to cover the London sky. They blocked out the moon, making the night even darker and keeping Horace and him in shadow as they stood on the roof of the Baroness's warehouse.

Per Estella's instructions, they were supposed to get inside and make it look like Cruella had broken in. Glancing at Horace, Jasper nodded. It was time. Tugging on the rope tied around his waist to make sure it was tight, Jasper took a breath and jumped down through the open skylight. Horace followed, though not quite as gracefully.

Landing in the middle of the designers' workroom, both boys stood still for a moment, their eyes scanning the area for any guards. The only light came from the open door to the security room. Through it, Jasper could make out the security guard. The man's head was down.

"Asleep on the job," Jasper said, pleased.

"You can't get good help these days," Horace replied.

Jasper nodded in agreement. Then, keeping an eye on the guard, he got to work. He walked to a mannequin and knocked it over. Like the first domino in a line, the mannequin toppled and hit the next, which fell into the next, and with a mighty crash, half a dozen dress forms fell to the ground.

Jasper's head snapped toward the guard. The man hadn't moved.

Taking a look around the room, Jasper gave Horace a satisfied nod. The fallen mannequins were sure to draw the Baroness's attention. They had done their job. Now it was time to get out of there. Grabbing their ropes, the boys climbed back out of the warehouse. It was time to get home before they risked anyone catching them.

Estella was nervous the next morning as she walked into the warehouse. Her conversation with the Baroness in the restaurant had played over and over in her head through the night. She was worried the woman was on to her. Estella just needed Cruella's identity to remain a secret for a little longer. And she needed Jasper and Horace's nighttime antics to help with the subterfuge. Would the Baroness believe that Cruella had broken in? Or believe that Estella was somehow involved?

She got her answer soon enough.

Upon making her way upstairs to the Baroness's office for her morning check-in, Estella found the woman standing, arms crossed, as her security guards loaded the new collection of dresses into a portable vault.

"What's going on?" Estella asked, hoping she sounded curious, not worried.

The Baroness didn't even look over before answering, "She tried to break in last night."

So the boys had done their job. That was good! But Estella needed to know more. "Who did?" she asked. *Please say Cruella, please say Cruella,* she added silently.

"Cruella."

Estella tried to keep the relief from her face. Her identity was still a secret.

"Makes sense," the Baroness went on, too absorbed in herself to notice Estella's reaction. "It's a stunning, ludicrously expensive gown. Cruella could never afford to make it. But this Cruella has no shame. She may steal my creation . . ." The Baroness paused and now met Estella's gaze. Her eyes were cold and full of challenge. "I mean, that would be a great idea, right, if you were her?"

Estella bit the inside of her cheek. She shouldn't have thought she was out of the woods yet. Clearly, the Baroness was probing, trying to get her to break. Estella didn't say anything, though. She simply smiled, hoping that it was neutral enough.

The Baroness shrugged. "Lucky I had my crack security team on high alert."

From what Jasper and Horace had told her about their little trip to the warehouse the night before, the "crack security team" was more like a "a sleepy security guard". But she thought it best not to mention that. "You're always a step ahead," Estella said instead.

"She's young and she tries hard," the Baroness said. "But she's met her match, and she'll see that soon."

With a wave of her hand, the last of the gowns was loaded into the vault. The large door shut with a clang, locking them all–including Estella's masterpiece–safely inside. Satisfied, the Baroness turned and left the room. The guards followed.

Estella stayed behind for a moment, her eyes glued to the vault. A young seamstress who had been hiding in the corner at the Baroness's command stood and started to leave as well. As she passed, Estella smiled–and lifted a pin from the cushion on the woman's wrist.

Let the Baroness believe that Cruella had met her match. It was easier to win when your opponent thought they had the upper hand. And Estella was going to win. No matter what.

Later that night, Estella sat hunched over her work space in the Lair. A row of dresses, her very own collection, were hanging on racks, waiting for Artie and the other dressmakers he'd brought in to help to steam them for the final "show". Turning off his steamer, Artie stretched, letting out a yawn. It was late. Estella knew she should follow Artie's lead and call it a night, but she had more work to do.

From the other room she heard the sound of the television as Horace watched a football match and talked to the Dalmatians. The big animals had become quite fond of Horace and spent most of their time glued to his side. Back before she had discovered the truth about the Baroness, Estella might very well have joined Horace. She would have cheered alongside him as their team played, maybe fallen asleep on the couch. But things were different now. She was different. All that mattered was getting her revenge.

Hearing footsteps, Estella didn't look up as Jasper put a cup of hot coffee down in front of her. "Night," he said softly.

She still didn't look up as she threaded her needle through the fabric in her hand. It was the last stitch on the last dress. The collection that she had worked on every night since Cruella's "birth" was nearly complete. She needed to focus, but she could feel Jasper's eyes on her.

"What?" she said.

"Where are you?" Jasper asked. He sounded worried. That bothered Estella.

"I'm right here," she said sharply. "Working toward a deadline."

Jasper shook his head. "I miss Estella," he said.

In the other room, Horace shouted happily as his team scored. The dogs joined in, barking. Estella turned, annoyed by the noise. She stared at the three dogs for a moment. "They would actually make fabulous coats," she said finally. Jasper looked horrified and she laughed. "I'm joking!" But the smile didn't meet her eyes and Jasper's expression didn't change. Jasper wanted to talk about things he missed? Well, Estella missed the Jasper who had a sense of humor. She wouldn't seriously harm a dog just to make a coat–even if they did have delicious spots.

Jasper sighed. "You know we've all had bad things happen to us," he said. "Me. You. We've always been there for each other."

Estella had had enough. She didn't need Jasper throwing her a guilt trip that night, of all nights. He was right.

Bad things had happened to them. So why couldn't he let her find a way to make them right? "That's all I'm asking," she snapped. "Is it so hard to support me? Back me up?"

"To help Estella? No," Jasper said. "That's easy. To help Cruella? It's a nightmare."

"That's that understatement thing you do!" Horace shouted from the other room. "It's worse than that."

Estella shot Horace a glare he couldn't see. Then she looked at Jasper. "Cruella gets things done," she said matter-of-factly. "Estella does not. And I have things to do." She turned back to the dress in her hand, hoping Jasper would take the hint. He didn't. He kept looking at her, with an expression she couldn't quite read but definitely didn't like. "So if you're done chatting . . . ?" she said leadingly. He still didn't move. Taking a page from the Baroness, Estella added, "And when I say *if*, I mean *you are*."

Jasper sighed, point–finally–taken. Turning to go, he stopped, as if he wanted to say more. But with a shake of his head, he headed toward the couch. *Good,* Estella thought as she turned back to her dress. *Peace at last.* A moment later, though, one of the Dalmatians walked in and sank down on a cushion near her.

Estella raised an eyebrow. The creature clearly hadn't heard her joke. "Aren't you brave?" she said. Then, with a smile, she turned back to her work.

Jasper could be upset with her. Horace could be scared of her. She didn't care. Not now. Soon enough they would see that she had been right all along–and that revenge would be the best heist they ever pulled off.

Chapter 21

It was a perfect night. London's normal damp and chill atmosphere had given way to a comfortable and pleasant evening. Even the stars were out—both the real ones and the celebrity version. Out in front of the Baroness's warehouse, a crowd of people had begun to gather, eager to see the reveal of the Baroness's latest collection. Rumors had been flying: The collection was going to be magnificent . . . her best yet. The collection was going to be terrible . . . outdated and rushed because of Cruella.

The Baroness ignored all the whispers. She knew that her collection was stellar. And the signature dress was going to blow away all the naysayers. Now, she just needed to get the collection out there.

Standing at the top of the stairs to her office, the Baroness watched as her minions rushed about, trying to get everything in its place before the guests would be allowed in. The vault had been moved down to the main floor of the warehouse and was now hidden behind a curtain, waiting for the moment its precious contents would be revealed. Per her orders, the designers' workroom had been transformed. The desks had been moved out and the boards taken down. In their place, lights had been hung, and where the desks had been now stood chairs that surrounded a long runway. It looked industrial and chic at the same time. The Baroness was pleased–or as pleased as she ever allowed herself to be. Even from inside, the Baroness sensed that the crowd was getting bigger and more restless. By now the VIP guests would be arriving. She would make them wait. It was a good reminder to them that she was in charge.

Beside her, John's eyes scanned the room. The valet's

face was, as usual, expressionless. To him, every worker below was a potential security risk or individual who might bother his boss. Typically, the Baroness liked his thoroughness, but right now she didn't care about all those workers. She cared about one.

"When 'Estella' arrives, escort her to my office and hold her there," she ordered. She looked suspiciously at him. "Can I trust you this time?"

He didn't bother to respond to the question. Instead, he told her again what he had been stating all day: Estella was not Cruella. There was no way she was capable of pulling off the Cruella stunts.

"Do I pay you for your opinion or obedience?" the Baroness said when he was done.

John opened his mouth and then thought better of it. He nodded. "I'll see it's done," he said.

The Baroness watched him walk down the stairs. How dare he question her? She had been putting the pieces together for days now. Matching moments and connecting the evidence. Cruella could be none other than Estella. It all made sense. She had studied Cruella's dresses and seen the same pattern in some of Estella's work. And she had never asked for Estella's references. She had just plucked her from that silly window display and plopped a dream job in her lap. She had no idea where the girl came from. Estella could easily have the evil mind needed to mess with her in such a way. But John could think whatever he wanted. It didn't matter as long as the Baroness got this show off without a hitch.

Hearing her name, she saw Jeffrey signaling to her from the bottom of the stairs. She sighed. Could these people do anything on their own? She made her way down toward her assistant and stopped in front of him. The man was visibly shaking, and his face was ghostly white.

"Speak!" the Baroness commanded.

But Jeffrey couldn't speak. He could just shake as he pointed to the curtain behind him. Sweeping past him, the Baroness brushed the curtain aside just enough to let her slip through. She didn't want the audience to see anything before it was time. And when she saw what was on the other side, she was glad for the precaution. A technician stood in front of the vault. He was fiddling with the control panel, which was flashing funny signs.

Following her in, Jeffrey finally found his voice. "There's

something wrong with the lock, Your Ladyship," he said.

The Baroness bit back a scream of frustration. She wasn't an idiot! She could see there was something wrong. The bigger issue wasn't what, but why? *Why* was it not working? The guests were arriving, and the show was due to start in less than an hour. "I don't care what you have to do, get it open!"

But an hour later, the vault was still unopened, and the crowd was growing restless. A who's who of the most important people in the fashion industry shifted on their uncomfortable chairs. They had come for a show, but so far, all they had seen was an empty runway. A few daring reporters jotted down observations and asked for quotes.

Peeking out from behind the curtain, the Baroness frowned. She didn't know the reporters and didn't have control of what people were saying. She needed to get this show going–now! Turning back to the technician, she pushed him aside. It was always up to her to get the job done. She reached down and got the blowtorch she had asked John to find. Handing it to the head of security, she gave him a nod and he fired it up. On the other side of the curtain, the guests gasped as they saw a bright red light appear.

The flame slowly cut through the hinges. The Baroness didn't take her eyes off the door as, inch by inch, the flame did its work. Finally, with a loud groan, the hinge broke and the door fell to the ground. They were in!

The Baroness sighed with relief as she stepped in front of the now open vault. But the feeling only lasted a moment. She was horrified when she saw, instead of dresses, a cloud of moths swarm out in a tornado of wings. As the people around her began to wave their hands and shriek, the Baroness's eyes flashed fire far hotter than any blowtorch could. Ignoring the workers and the moths, she stared inside the depths of the vault.

Her dresses, each and every one, were destroyed. Holes had been eaten into every piece of fabric, every sleeve, every bodice, every train. It was a complete and utter disaster. As her rage built, the Baroness looked at the signature gown. Placed in the middle of all the others, it was still beautiful, but there was something different. It no longer seemed to glow and shine. Watching, she saw one of the beads begin to shake. A moment later, it broke open and a moth crawled out.

Fury filled the Baroness. The beads weren't beads at all! They had been cocoons for moths–hundreds and hundreds of cocoons. Neatly sewn onto the dress by that wretched Estella, they had been ticking time bombs. And now they had exploded and wreaked their havoc.

As the moths made their way out further into the warehouse, the guests began to scream. Chairs screeched as people rushed to get away from the infestation. Within moments, the warehouse was empty.

The Baroness's show was over before it could even begin.

The Baroness was sure she could not get any madder. Seeing her collection ruined made her blood hiss.

And then she stepped foot outside the warehouse.

Her blood went from steaming to boiling.

As she made her way onto the street, she saw the last of her guests fleeing her show. Like the moths they were running from, they seemed drawn to the lights that were pulsating and glowing from inside Regent's Park. The Baroness frowned. What was going on?

Heading upstairs toward the large balcony outside her office, the Baroness looked out at the park. A huge crowd had formed around the tiered fountain. All eyes were glued to the show happening in front of them—a fantastic, loud and raucous, bright and bold punk rock pop-up fashion show. Models strutted around the fountain, decked out in street-hip clothing that was the exact opposite of the classic haute couture pieces of the Baroness's collection.

The crowd cheered, getting louder with the reveal of each over-the-top outfit. As the Baroness scanned the faces gathered, her rage built. These were *her* guests, the elite of the fashion world, who were supposed to be attending her show. Instead, they were standing out in the chilly night air, watching this neon nightmare—and enjoying it. Her eyes kept roaming, and she spotted Anita Darling snapping photographs beside a pair of rough-and-tumble boys. Probably homeless, the Baroness thought coldly.

"It's got a good beat."

Her head whipped to the right. John had come and was standing next to her, his eyes on the crowd in the park. She flashed him a furious look. She was really going to think long and hard about firing him. He should know better than to say anything positive about the debacle unfolding in front of her.

Just as she opened her mouth to snap at him, a figure appeared at the end of the makeshift runway. A beam of light illuminated the figure as she strode down the long walkway and, upon reaching the end, spun first left, then right. The light continued to follow, just close enough to give glimpses of the outfit but not close enough to reveal a face. The figure twirled and strutted to the eager crowd and, finally, leaned into a bow. When she arose, the light fell on her face. The Baroness gasped. It was Cruella! And she was wearing a black-and-white spotted fur coat—a coat that looked like it was made out of Dalmatian! As the crowd gasped and cheered, Cruella lifted her arm, soaking in the praise.

"This is the future!" she shouted. As her words echoed over the park, in the distance was the familiar wail of police sirens.

Instantly, one of the boys who appeared homeless flipped a switch and the lights went down. A moment later, the music went off. The models, the crowd, and Cruella scattered, disappearing into the darkness. The two homeless boys hesitated, looking around as if to make sure nothing was left behind. The Baroness watched the pair closely. Perhaps there was more to those boys than she had thought.

"She killed my dogs . . ." the Baroness whispered. Even

with the lights off, the image of Cruella in the Dalmatian coat was seared in her brain. The rebel had gone too far. It was one thing to mess with her; it was an entirely different thing to mess with her dogs.

The Baroness was done with the little battles. Cruella wanted a fight? She was going to get a war. Turning to John, she ordered him to follow the boys. She had a feeling that where they went, Cruella might follow.

Chapter 22

Cruella was on cloud nine. Her show had gone off perfectly. Even if the police had caught wind of it, they hadn't gotten there in time to wreck her final appearance. She knew that somewhere the Baroness had been watching—that had been her plan all along—and she just wished she could have seen the look on the woman's face when she appeared wearing her Dalmatian coat.

She knew that Jasper and Horace were probably angry at her for not joining them and going back to the Lair, but she didn't care. She was too wired to sleep, too happy to face their sour faces and words of warning. She knew that she was facing off against a monster and should be careful. But that night she just wanted to relax. Her stomach growled. *And eat,* she added to herself. She wanted to relax and eat.

Glancing down the street, she saw an Indian restaurant with the OPEN sign still on. Perfect. She headed over and took her place in line. It was surprisingly busy for the middle of the night. She noticed a TV on in the corner. A news anchor was breaking into the nightly news. Cruella watched the bulletin with interest. "In the biggest fashion scandal since Yves Saint Laurent was accidently declared dead," the anchor was saying, "the Baroness Von Hellman has canceled her show after a swarm of moths ate her entire collection." Estella smiled. She was still pleased with that move. No one could ever have expected that she would know a species of moth that encased itself in a glittering "bead" cocoon. If she could have, she would have patted herself on the back. As it was, her hands were now full of Indian food, so she instead turned her attention back to the TV.

"Maybe the moths knew something," the fashion

reporter said, "because the House of Baroness is looking positively old and musty next to tonight's explosion of the new couture icon, Cruella, in what can only be described as a fashion riot in Regent's Park."

Estella didn't need to hear any more. "New couture icon." Brilliant. It was everything she had dreamed of and more. It couldn't have worked out better. The thought made her feel momentarily guilty. She wouldn't have been able to do it without Jasper, Horace, and Artie. Turning back to the counter, she ordered some more food. They might be mad, but who could stay mad when she brought home Indian?

Floating out of the restaurant and down the street, she quickly made her way back to the Lair. She couldn't wait to see the boys. She wanted to hear everything. Who had they seen? What news did they have? How did they get away without getting noticed? The bags of takeaway swung by her side and she had to restrain herself from skipping up the stairs when she got to the Lair.

She pushed open the door and lifted her arms triumphantly. "The queen is dead! Long live the queen . . ." As she flicked on the lights, her voice trailed off.

Horace and Jasper were tied to chairs, their hands bound and their mouths gagged. The flesh around Horace's eye was turning purple, and blood was caked in the corner of his mouth. He had clearly been beaten up. Behind them stood two big men, their fists clenched, their expressions cold.

"Cruella."

Hearing her name–or rather her other name–Estella slowly turned. The Baroness stood behind her, flanked by the Dalmatians. Light from the large window cast her face in shadow, but Estella could feel the venom pouring from the other woman. In the cage they had used to transport the Dalmatians, Buddy and Wink now whined nervously. Clearly, the woman had put two and two together and followed Jasper and Horace back to the Lair. After all their careful planning, they had been caught.

"Wow," Estella said when she had collected herself. There was no use pretending to be nice or subservient anymore. "You really are a psycho."

"Why, thank you," the Baroness said. "Nice of you to say. You showed promise. As did Estella." Estella saw that the Baroness was clutching her red wig.

Estella's eyes shifted from the Baroness to her friends. They were watching, nervous and a bit scared. She didn't blame them. They all knew what the Baroness was capable of, but she wasn't going to back down without a fight.

"This is between us," she said. "Let Jasper and Horace–imbeciles that they are for letting you follow them–go." She heard her friends protest behind their gags, but she ignored them. They had to know she wasn't really upset. She was scared.

The Baroness shrugged. "Oh, I will," she said. "They'll be going to prison."

"For what? Dognapping?" Estella cracked.

The corner of the Baroness's mouth lifted, and amusement seemed to fill her eyes. The look made Estella nervous, and rightly so. "Your murder," she replied, correcting her.

"No one will believe that," Estella said, though she knew she didn't sound convincing.

"Well, we'll have to add your charred body to the mix to help the believability factor," the Baroness said with a shrug. As she spoke, one of the bodyguards came around from behind Jasper and Horace and grabbed Cruella. While she struggled, the other bodyguard dragged

Horace and Jasper out of the room. Estella was helpless to do anything as the bodyguard slammed her into a chair and tied her down.

With Estella and the boys secured, the bodyguards grabbed big containers of gasoline and sloshed the liquid over the floor, furniture, and walls of the Lair. It would take only moments for the place to go up in flames once the match was lit.

"You're going to kill me because I upstaged you?" Estella asked, struggling against her restraints.

"Uh-huh," the Baroness replied. Beside her, the Dalmatians struggled on their leashes, trying to get to Buddy and Wink. It was heartbreaking to watch, and for a moment, Estella felt bad for the creatures. They weren't evil–their owner was. With a shout, the Baroness jerked them back and ordered them to sit.

Estella shook her head. She was about to be aflame. There was no reason not to put all the cards on the table. "I know you killed my mother," she said. She waited, expecting astonishment to cross the Baroness's face.

Instead, the woman just gave her a blank look. "You'll have to be more specific."

"What?" Estella said, shocked. Did the woman mean to imply she had killed other people?

Apparently so. "Who exactly?" the Baroness said. "You'll need to narrow it down for me."

"On the cliff," Estella said. "You called your dogs on her."

The Baroness nodded as she made the connection. "Okay, I'm with you now," she said. Then she shrugged. "So you're peeved about that. Hence the show you've put on?"

Estella blinked rapidly. Just when she thought the Baroness couldn't get worse, she did. The woman was a terrible human being. A monster. A monster with no conscience. Rage and sadness rushed through Estella in equal measure. How different would her life have been if she and her mum had just never gone to see the Baroness? The rage took over and Estella pulled at the rope against her. "I'm going to kill you!" she screamed. "And your dogs!"

The Baroness reached into her pocket and pulled out a lighter. In one smooth move, she flicked it and a flame burst from the top. "I'm waiting," she said.

A sense of calm filled Estella as she watched the woman holding the flame. It was mesmerizing and powerful to know that there was nothing she could do or say now that would matter. Her life would go up in flames. So she might as well mess with the Baroness as much as she could until then.

She looked at the security guards. "Would you gents let me go for a moment?" she asked. "I'm sure she's a terrible boss. I'd like to offer you both a new position. Full medical. Four weeks holiday." No surprise: the men started to think about it.

Seeing their looks, the Baroness shouted, "Enough!" She stared back at Estella. Her eyes lingered on the girl's black-and-white tresses. "Just double-checking. That is your natural hair color?"

"Yes," Estella said. "Why?"

"No reason," the Baroness said. Then, with a flick of her wrist, she sent the lighter into the middle of the gasoline. Flames rose up instantly. "Goodbye, Cruella." She turned to one of the guards and ordered him to tip off the press. Then, as the flames grew, she added, "I'd love them to know you went out in a blaze of glory." With a wave of her hand and a tug on the leash, the Baroness left, dragging the Dalmatians with her and leaving Estella to die.

CHAPTER TWENTY-TWO

Estella coughed and choked as smoke filled the air. It was one thing to act bold and brave in front of the Baroness, but it was different when faced with fire. The Lair was an inferno. Through the thickening black, Estella watched in horror as her work went up in flames. The costumes she had made over the years, the sketches she had dreamed up at night, the furniture she and the guys had painstakingly dragged up to help make the place a home. It was all being destroyed. And soon Estella would join it. She thought of Jasper and Horace and Wink and Buddy. Her family. They were going to be destroyed, too. The boys would go to jail and the dogs would die.

All because of her.

Coughing, Estella fought to stay conscious. But it was too hard. Her eyes began to close, and her breathing became shallower. Struggling to open her eyes, she saw that Buddy and Wink, through the bars of their cage, were trying to help her, biting and gnawing at the ropes that bound her. Then she spotted something in the flames, glinting from a pile of poop. She tried to shake her head and clear her vision, but the movement was too much for her.

She slipped into unconsciousness. But just before the darkness completely took her, she could have sworn she felt arms wrap around her and lift her into the air. She tried to speak, but no words came. Instead, she let the darkness envelop her.

Estella's throat hurt. Her eyes burned. Her body ached. Her lungs felt like they were on fire. And it felt like dirty water was being swiped across her face.

Slowly and carefully, she opened her eyes. Buddy was beside her, licking her face while Wink sat on top of the couch she was lying on. His little face looked worried and he whined when he saw her. She sat up, a fresh wave of pain flooding through her body and lungs as she took a shaky breath.

Where was she?

It was definitely not the Lair. In a flash, she remembered the flames and the Baroness's evil laugh as she left her to die. So what had happened? The room she was in was cozy and warm, the colors muted and decidedly male.

CHAPTER TWENTY-TWO

Hearing footsteps, Estella pushed nervously back against the pillows. She was too weak to fight or run. A moment later, the Baroness's valet, John, appeared in the door to the living room, a cup in his hand.

"Tea, Miss Cruella?" he said when he saw she was awake.

Estella shook her head. Was she still unconscious? "You?" She sat up, grabbing her jacket, which had been placed over her like a blanket, and hugging it to her chest. "Why? Why am I alive?"

"Because I dragged you out of the flames and smoke before they consumed you," he said simply. As though that explained everything. But it just left Estella with more questions.

"Why?" she asked again. "You work for *her*."

John sighed and sat down on a chair across from Estella. He leaned back, legs crossed. In his cozy flat, he seemed different. He was gentler, Estella realized, and not nearly as scary. She waited for him to answer, her mind racing with this sudden change in dynamics.

Finally, he spoke. "I knew your mother and . . ." His voice got tight. Estella stared at him. He had known her mother?

Again, she had questions, but he went on. "I couldn't let that happen. I have something for you." Reaching into his pocket, he pulled out her mother's necklace, which sparkled as it dangled from his fingers, and offered it to her.

"You found it!" Estella gasped, taking it delicately in her hand.

He nodded. "In the fire. I assure you it has been bleached repeatedly." He gave Estella a smile. "May I show you something?" He held out his hand.

Estella passed the necklace back to John. Carefully, he began to unscrew the top of the locket. A moment later there was a click and he pulled out a small, thin key.

"I didn't know it had a key," Estella said, shocked. "What's it for?"

John didn't answer right away. Instead, he took the key and made his way to the fireplace. Taking down an antique box, he carried it over and placed it down on the coffee table in front of Estella. He handed her the key.

"This," he said.

Estella hesitated and then slipped the key inside the lock. It fit. As she turned, the lock popped open. Lifting the lid, Estella saw a birth certificate. She scanned the paper and saw the words *baby girl* and, beside *mother*, the name Baroness Von Hellman.

"The Baroness has a kid?" Estella asked, shocked.

John nodded. "Yes," he said. "You."

"Me what?" Estella asked, using the words to give her brain time to catch up with John's statement. Was John messing with her? Was this part of the Baroness's plan? Let her think she was going to die and then have her lackey tell her that her whole life was a lie? But looking up, she saw that John's face was very serious. This wasn't a joke. Or at least not the funny kind.

"Let me walk you through it." Closing the lid, John took a deep breath. "The Baroness never wanted children," he explained. "She's a true narcissist; she can't love anything but herself. She'd lied and cheated to get the old Baron to marry her." That part Estella could believe. She imagined the Baroness, young and beautiful, charming her way into the Baron's heart–and wealth. John went on. "So when she found out she was pregnant, she was far from happy. The Baron was so excited about the coming baby that he changed his will. Left everything to the child."

Estella knew that that wouldn't have sat well with

the Baroness. Not if what she wanted was the money all to herself. But to believe that she was the daughter of the Baron and Baroness Von Hellman? It didn't make sense. It just couldn't be.

John saw the look of doubt in her eyes. "You are her daughter," he said. "I was there when you were born." He had watched on the dark, stormy night as Estella came kicking and screaming into the world. The Baron had been away on business and the Baroness had used that to her advantage. She had barely even looked at the child before ordering John to "take care of it".

So he had. He had brought the crying baby out of the room and done the only thing he could think of: give the baby, Estella, to one of the housemaids–a young woman named Catherine. When Estella heard her mum's name, her eyes welled with tears. In the dark of the night, John had given Catherine what little money he had–and the necklace–and told her to go, make a new life for herself and the baby as far away from the mansion as she could get.

When the Baron returned, the Baroness told him the child had died. "That's what she expected of me," John said softly, his voice full of emotion. "So I let her believe it was true. The old Baron, he wasted away. Some said it was grief."

Estella's heart ached. So much sadness and death had been caused because of her. And she had never known any of it. She wanted to reach out and hold John's hand, find any human connection, but the man was lost in the memory and his own grief.

"After he died, the Baroness discovered he never changed his will back. But since everyone thought you were dead . . . it went to her instead." He stopped, his story almost over. He looked up and met Estella's eyes. "The point I'm trying to make is that you are the rightful heir to the Baron's entire fortune. The mansion, the title . . . everything."

For a long moment, Estella just stared at John. Her mind was racing, her heart breaking. But slowly, anger replaced the sadness. "That psycho *cannot* be my mother!" she shouted.

"I know, it's a shock," John said, calm in the face of her rage. He was used to it, after all.

Estella got to her feet, her jacket falling to the ground, her eyes blazing. It wasn't a shock, it was a nightmare. She felt her breath coming in gasps. She needed to get out of this room and away from the story she had just heard. As John begged her to stop and stay, Estella ran out the door and onto the street.

She didn't know where she was going. She just needed to get as far from John as possible. Not that it was his fault. Not really. He had only been trying to help her, but his words kept running through her mind, piercing her heart.

She didn't stop until she found herself back at the fountain in Regent's Park. Exhausted, she slumped down on the same bench she had slept on her first night in London. In the early morning, the fountain was not running, so Estella just stared at the still water, wishing her own life was as calm.

Her nemesis was her real mother. And her real mother had killed her other mother. It was all so confusing. No wonder her mum–her fake one, she supposed–had always been telling her to "tone it down" and "try to fit in". She was probably scared all along that Estella would become like the Baroness–cruel and heartless. Estella fought back tears. The whole time, her mum had just been trying to love her into shape. "And I really tried to be that," Estella said aloud, her voice soft as she spoke to her mother's memory. "Because I love you. But the truth is I'm not sweet Estella, try as I might. I never was." As she went on, her voice became steadier, stronger, more self-assured. "I'm Cruella. Born brilliant, born bad, and maybe a little mad. That's me, but I'm not like her. I'm better."

Getting to her feet, Estella took a deep breath. The truth was out there now. Estella was armed with the one fact that could topple the Baroness. And while she knew the woman who loved her and raised her wouldn't approve, Estella was done trying to be anyone but who she was.

Estella was dead. Let everyone think she had gone up in flames. But Cruella was alive. And Cruella was going to avenge, revenge, and destroy the Baroness Von Hellman—for her mum, for the Baron, for John, and for her own lost childhood and the life she might have had.

Chapter 23

Inside the police station, Jasper lay on his back on a dirty cot. Across the cell, Horace lay on his own cot. The Baroness had been true to her word and had them arrested for Estella's murder. With the Lair an inferno and the headlines already announcing her death, the police didn't question it. They locked Jasper and Horace up with only the vague promise of a trial.

Blowing his nose, Horace rolled over and looked at Jasper. "I can't believe she's dead," he said.

CHAPTER TWENTY-THREE

Jasper couldn't believe it, either. Images of Estella, the fun, feisty girl he had met years earlier, flashed through his mind. "Let's just remember Estella," he finally said, "and forget Cruella."

Before he could say more, he heard a rumbling sound coming from outside. "Do you hear that?" he asked. Both boys sat up. The noise was getting louder. Out in the bull-pen, the officers took notice of the sound as well. Looking out the front doors, one of the men shouted just as a huge dump truck slammed into the building. Glass and furniture went flying as police officers flung themselves out of the way.

A moment later, the driver's side door of the truck opened. Cruella, dressed as a garbageman, complete with a fake mustache, leaned out. As the officers regained their composure, they focused their attention on Cruella. They didn't notice Wink hop out of the cab and head inside.

Giving the men a wave, Cruella got back in the cab and threw it into reverse. As the truck pulled out, the police jumped into their police cruisers and gave chase.

Standing in his cell, fingers wrapped around the bars, Jasper listened to the chaos, unsure of what was happening.

A moment later, he shouted happily as Wink trotted into view. Jumping to his feet, Horace joined Jasper at the cell door.

"Wink!" Horace cried happily. "You ain't barbecued!"

Jasper looked down at the little dog. No, he most certainly was not. And better still, he was carrying the keys to their escape. Tied to his back was a lock-picking kit. Reaching down, Jasper grabbed the kit and got to work while Horace showered his pup with pats. In seconds, the door swung open and Jasper and Horace walked out.

In the chaos, none of the officers even noticed as the two prisoners made their way into the street. Night had fallen, aiding in their escape. It also helped that outside the station was utter mayhem. Cars were backed up and down the street. A huge pile of stinking garbage was lying in the middle of the road, blocking anyone from coming or going.

Slipping into an alley, Jasper, Horace, and Wink walked quickly, putting as much distance between themselves and the station as they could. They had just turned down another dark street when a garbage truck pulled up beside them. It stopped, and Cruella rolled down the window.

"Want a ride?" she asked, smiling.

Jasper didn't return the smile. He had had a feeling the breakout was Cruella's doing. And for a moment, he had been happy that his friend was still alive. But now that he had had a walk in the fresh air to think about it, he was angry all over again. The only reason they were in that spot in the first place was because of her. "We'll walk," he said.

Horace was not as upset. "You're alive!" he said happily, moving toward the truck.

Jasper stopped him. "You nearly got us killed," he said, letting his anger out. "You treated us like the help." He nodded to his friend. "Keep walking, Horace."

Thankfully, Horace didn't question him. They continued down the street.

"You'll get caught by the cops," Cruella called out.

"We did fine before you turned up," Jasper shouted over his shoulder. "We'll do fine without you." He knew his words were harsh, but he no longer cared.

Horace, ever loyal, nodded. "You called me 'imbecile,'" he added. "I don't know what that means, but I'm pretty sure it's bad."

"It's not terrible," Cruella said, though it didn't sound convincing.

Jasper ignored her. He was tired and hungry. He wanted something to eat, and then he wanted to find a place to sleep. He headed toward a café. Behind him, he heard the garbage truck's engine rev, and a moment later the vehicle pulled up beside them.

Cruella stared down at them, her face awash in pain. Jasper hesitated. He had only seen her look this upset when she found out the truth about her mother's death. What had happened now?

"There's no easy way to say this," she said, as if reading his silent question. "The Baroness is my birth mother."

Jasper and Horace stopped in their tracks, struck silent by the revelation.

A moment later, Horace spoke. "I have so many follow-up questions."

Jasper sighed. It looked like they were going to take that ride after all.

Jasper and Horace sat on the couch in John's living room, a plate of crumpets lying uneaten in front of them. Well, mostly uneaten. Horace had helped himself to several. They had listened as Estella filled them in on what she had found out: the truth about what the Baroness had done and the lengths she had gone to keep her hands on the Baron's money.

"The minute she knows I'm alive," Estella finished, "she'll try to kill me. We're in a kill-or-be-killed situation here."

Jasper shook his head. He felt bad for Estella. But he was still hurt. "She's a homicidal maniac and you're not," he said.

"We don't know that yet," Estella said, trying to lighten the situation. "I'm still young."

"Funny," Jasper said flatly. "Or it would be funny if I was sure you were being funny."

Estella moved closer, and Jasper shifted away. She sighed. "I *am* joking," she said. "But we have to stop her. I have a plan, but I can't do it without you guys."

Horace looked up, crumpet crumbs on his cheeks. "Finally!" he said. "She gets it. I'm essential to any plan."

Estella gave him a warm smile. "I went a bit mad, and I'm so sorry," she said, her voice husky. Jasper could see she was trying to keep it together and he started to soften. "You're my family. All I have . . ." she continued.

The last of Jasper's resolve faded. Jasper sighed. "All right, all right," he said. "What's the plan?"

Estella didn't hesitate. "The Baroness's charity gala is this weekend." She paused to see if Jasper was listening. He was, even though he already didn't like the sound of this. "We'll need all the guests' home addresses and measurements, Artie's tribe of dressmakers, a black cape, pots of paint, several boned corsets, and–"

Her list was interrupted by the arrival of John. Jasper stiffened.

"John," Estella said, clearly not surprised by his appearance. "This is my family. They'll be staying awhile."

John nodded while Jasper looked back and forth between him and Estella. It had only been a night since the fire and yet everything seemed to have changed. Well, almost everything.

"You're out of crumpets," Horace said, pointing to the now empty plate.

Jasper smiled wryly at his friend's comment. Nothing fazed Horace. They were in way over their heads and Jasper didn't like this plan. But at least for now he was going to have to go with the flow.

CHAPTER TWENTY-THREE

They got right to work. John's flat became base camp. In a matter of hours, any sign of tweed or wool was replaced with colorful fabric, and every surface was covered with sewing material. Artie's band of merry dressmakers stood in front of dress forms, humming and chatting as they clipped, ripped, and pinned. A few people took notes as Estella barked out orders, the commander of the army. Every once in a while, she would stop to check a dress or help with a pinning. The ultimate goal? Boxing up dozens upon dozens of dresses of her own design—each stamped with the House of Baroness label.

While she took care of the clothes, John snagged the client files from the Baroness's office. It didn't take much to find them. The Baroness believed John had her best interests at heart, so she let him put away the paperwork.

With files in hand and dresses made and packed, it was time for Jasper and Horace to play their part. They loaded the van up with the boxes—also embossed with the Baroness's logo—and made their rounds, stopping at estate after estate. Each time, Horace got out and hand delivered the beautiful box. And each time, the woman who received the package squealed with delight as she opened the box to find a one-of-a-kind gown and a note: *Please wear this, with my compliments.* In just a few days, the deliveries were done. The first part of the plan was complete. It was easy, Jasper thought as he and Horace drove back to the flat. Like taking candy from a baby.

And that made Jasper nervous.

Or rather, more nervous than usual.

As the sun set on the night of the gala, Jasper made his way to Estella's room. The window was open, leading out to the small fire escape and the stairs to the rooftop of John's flat. Looking up, Jasper saw Estella perched on the brick wall, looking out at London's skyline. It was aglow in red and orange and, for once, seemed peaceful. From the roof, the busy sounds of the street faded, and the air smelled fresher.

"Hey," he called up, climbing through the window and joining her. "Big night."

"Indeed, it is."

Jasper stared at her for a moment, wondering what she was thinking. Ever since the fire and discovering the truth about her mother, Estella had been different. More distant. He knew she had gone to see a lawyer about the Baron's will, but she hadn't said anything. Her focus had been completely on the gala.

"You sure about this?" he asked.

She nodded.

"You know you can't kill her, Estella," he said, voicing the worry that had been in his head.

She shrugged. "Can't or shouldn't?"

That was not the response he wanted. Frustrated, he ran a hand through his hair and took a few calming breaths. "I know you're in pain," he said. "And she caused it. But killing her isn't going to make that go away."

"I won't," Estella said, for a moment sounding like his old friend. Jasper felt a flash of hope. But then she went on. "Unless I really, really have to."

Jasper sighed. He couldn't tell if she was being serious or not, but he could tell that his words were falling on deaf ears. Turning to him, she met his gaze and her eyes softened. "Thanks for helping me," she said quietly.

"It's difficult to say no to you sometimes," he admitted.

"It's one of the things I love about you," she said.

Jasper flushed, unsure how to respond. Luckily, he was saved by the bell . . . or rather a honk. Looking down into the alley below, he saw Horace pulling up in the car they had stolen from the Baroness months ago. Horace had been fixing it up, and now it gleamed, black and white. Every inch was polished to a fine shine.

Horace got out and waved up to them. "When I washed it, I noticed the name," he said. "You know what this car's called? A devil."

Jasper laughed. "It's DeVille, mate," he said, correcting Horace.

Horace shrugged, but Estella smiled. "I like that," she said, jumping up. It was time. They had the ride; they had the plan. They were ready. "Shall we go do this?"

Getting up, Jasper nodded. Like he had said, sometimes, even when he didn't like it, he just couldn't say no to her.

I want her caught before she's seen," the Baroness ordered. "Everyone thinks she's dead. She needs to be that way by the end of the night."

The man nodded. "I have a special treat for her," he said. He reached down and pulled a stun gun from his utility belt. "It'll put a shock through her and leave her incapacitated."

Like a child reaching for a toy, the Baroness took the stun gun. She turned it over in her hand, examining it. And then she stunned him. The huge man shouted and fell to the ground. She did it again, this time stunning a passing maid. "I could do this all day!" she said happily. Then the smile disappeared and she was once again the serious Viking warrior. "Go and find her, you idiots!" she said to the remaining guards, throwing them the stun gun.

Stepping away from the mirror, she went to her dresser and slipped her dog whistle on her left wrist. "Why am I the only one who is competent?" she said as John handed her the dogs' leashes.

"It must be tiring," the valet said. "It should be a memorable night, Baroness," he added as they began to leave the room.

The Baroness shot him a look. Indeed, it most certainly would be. It was time for the final battle to begin.

Outside Hellman Hall, the guests had begun to arrive. As ordered, the massive security detail hired by the Baroness had their eyes peeled for anyone with black-and-white hair who matched Cruella's description.

But there was a problem: every woman who got out of every car had black-and-white hair. First one, then another arrived, each wearing a different gown but sporting a black-and-white wig. It was impossible to tell one from the other: they all looked like Cruella.

In the security room, the guards watched on monitors, confused as they spotted Cruella on the East Lawn, then in the ballroom, then in the rose garden. There were dozens of them. Security didn't know what to do.

Pulling up in the DeVille, Jasper stopped in front of the doors. Looking around at the confusion unfolding, he had to smile. Cruella really had outdone herself this time. The party hadn't even started, and things were already out of control. Turning, he looked at Horace in the back seat.

He, like all the other guests, was dressed as Cruella–down to the wig and a fake fur wrap. Nestled in the wrap was Wink; Buddy hid at his feet.

Maneuvering himself awkwardly out of the car and stumbling a bit in his heels, Horace headed inside while Jasper parked the car. A few moments later, Jasper joined the throng of bodyguards frantically trying to find the "real" Cruella. He had replaced his valet uniform with a security guard uniform. As he made his way through the crowd, John appeared and slipped him an earpiece.

"All teams, all teams," he said into the piece. "Baroness requires everyone in the library . . . now. She's angry, boys."

He smiled as the guards he could spot went instantly still and their faces paled. Then they all sprinted toward the mansion and headed inside. Jasper nodded, satisfied. If things were going smoothly inside, Horace would be waiting for all the guards to file in the library. Once they were contained, he would shut the doors and lock them inside, leaving the mansion wide open for Cruella. He knew his job was to stay where he was, but a part of him really wanted to watch Horace give it to whoever dared go up against him. He could easily imagine them underestimating the portly Horace–especially in a dress. But Horace never ceased to surprise him, and he would do the same to the guards. By this point, Jasper guessed that Horace had locked them in, and was now meeting up with Artie for the next phase of the plan.

Yes, he was sure of it. Now it was time for him to get in position.

Sweeping down the long hallway, the Baroness made her way toward the grand ballroom. The Dalmatians followed her. "Time for my entrance, my dears," she said to the dogs. They whined in answer. Spotting Jeffrey up ahead, she gave him the briefest of nods as she brushed past him.

Jeffrey ran to catch up. His breathing was shallow as he struggled to find his words. "Baroness," he finally got out, "I was coming to–"

The Baroness's steps slowed as she turned to look at the weaselly little man. "Is she here?" she asked.

"Well . . ." Jeffrey said. A look from the Baroness had him finish hurriedly. "That's the problem–"

The Baroness didn't wait for him to finish. Shoving

him aside, she rushed toward the ballroom. Reaching the top of the stairs, she grabbed a glass of champagne from a tray and moved to position, ready to present herself to her adoring guests. But when she looked down into the room, she gasped in horror. She was staring at a sea of Cruellas. Every guest, male or female, was wearing a distinctive wig. It was her worst nightmare come to vivid, black-and-white life. Swallowing back the bile that rose in her throat, she lifted her glass.

"Thank you all for coming!" she said, thinking quickly about how to spin this in her favor. "What a great tribute to our dear friend"–her voice took on a brittle edge–"who will never return. Sadly." She raised her glass. "To Cruella!"

Below her, the crowd burst into applause and tilted back their own glasses. The Baroness was furious. But she kept a smile plastered on her face as she descended the staircase and made her way through the crowd. Her eyes scanned every guest, looking beyond the wig to see if she could spot the real Cruella's face. While she didn't find her, she did see Anita Darling. The young woman had a smug look on her face, which only infuriated the Baroness even more. She had *known* that Anita was in on it. Her look just confirmed it. She stalked over and stopped inches from Anita.

"Where is she?" the Baroness hissed.

Anita shrugged. "She seems to be there"–she pointed to a guest–"and there. I think she's everywhere."

Biting back a scream, the Baroness turned her back on Anita. She would find the girl. And then she would make her pay.

Chapter 25

From the balcony, Estella looked down as the Baroness pushed her way through her guests, and she took pleasure in the look of disgust the Baroness couldn't keep from her face. It thrilled Estella to her core. After everything the Baroness had done to destroy her, she had failed. And now she was the one whose evening—and life—was going to be ruined.

Estella slipped into the crowd and made her way closer. As she walked, she pulled a small silver hatpin from her hair and held it in her hand. The others had done their part. Now it was her turn. She slowed as she saw the Baroness approach John. Getting close enough to hear, she listened in.

"Not exactly a Viking gala," John said, nodding to the guests.

The Baroness sneered at him. "She's here."

"It would appear so, Baroness," John replied.

Moving in behind her, Estella reached out and swiftly pricked the Baroness's arm with the pin. Before the Baroness could even react, Estella had moved back into the crowd, undistinguishable from her sea of look-alikes. She now held the dog whistle she had swiped from the Baroness's other wrist while she'd distracted her with the pin prick. As Estella walked away, she heard the Baroness tell John to find her. She smiled. The Baroness could look all she wanted. She wasn't going to find Cruella.

With the whistle in hand, Estella made her way to the back of the mansion. Making sure no one was looking, she slipped into a bathroom. She took off her gown and straightened the frumpy dress beneath. Then she put her red wig on her head, completing the transformation back into Estella. She was ready.

Now, she just needed the Baroness to come to her. She squeezed the dog whistle in her hand. She had that covered as well. Going toward the doors to the garden, she looked at the large wall of glass. A memory from that horrible night years earlier flashed through her mind: it was of her staring out the glass as the storm raged and her mother and the Baroness spoke on the cliff's edge. The same anxiety she had felt that night filled her now. But alongside it was rage. And the rage was what pushed her out the door and toward the cliff.

When she was in place, she put the whistle to her lips and blew.

She didn't have to wait long. The whistle worked and within minutes, she heard the telltale barking of the Baroness's Dalmatians. Then they appeared, leashes dragging behind them as they raced out of the mansion and across the grass toward her. She saw the Baroness silhouetted from the light of the house as she called out to the dogs to "get her". Behind her stood the guards, who had finally broken out of the library. They were at the ready, but the Baroness ordered them to stand down.

Estella didn't move as the dogs raced at her. Closer and closer they got, barking wildly. And then, when they were just a foot away, they stopped. Sitting down, they wagged their tails happily. *Good doggies,* she mouthed.

The Baroness strode toward Estella, her chain mail clinking as she approached.

Estella didn't move. She had waited so long for this moment–when she would have the upper hand. She wasn't going to let the Baroness see one bit of weakness on her part. The older woman might have been the one in armor, but Estella had spent a long time building up her own suit of protection.

Finally, the Baroness was in front of her. She stopped, hands on hips. "Hello, Cruella," she said.

"Hello, Mother," Estella replied, pleased to see the Baroness flinch ever so slightly at being addressed that way.

"You can take the ridiculous disguise off," the Baroness said, waving at the "Estella" outfit.

Estella looked down at her dress and then touched her red hair. Then she shrugged. Instead of removing her own wig, she looked back at the house. "I hate to ruin your party," she said. "But I came to evict you. This is my property."

"Don't be ridiculous," the Baroness snapped, though her voice trembled slightly.

Estella smiled. The Baroness could say what she wanted, but Estella had done her research. She had talked to the lawyers. She knew how wrong the Baroness was, but she would revel in spelling it out for her. Pulling the small key from her locket out of her pocket, she held it up. "This is the key from the locket that opened the box that my birth certificate was in," she said. She spoke slowly, to make sure the Baroness heard every word. "And you just thought it was pretty."

For a moment, the Baroness was silent as she took it all in. Then, slowly, she nodded. "It all makes sense now."

"What?" Estella asked. Looking behind the Baroness, she tried to see what was going on inside the mansion. If the plan was still on track, at this very moment, John and Jasper would be ushering the guests outside for the evening's "special entertainment". Not seeing any movement yet, she turned back to the Baroness. She needed to draw this out.

"That you're so extraordinary," she replied. "Of course, you're mine."

The words stunned Estella, and for a moment, she didn't know what to say. Taking her silence as a gesture to go on, the Baroness continued. Overhead, thunder rumbled, and in the distance, lightning flashed.

"I've longed for someone in my life who was . . . as good as me," she said.

"What about someone better?" Estella said, recovering her voice.

The Baroness smiled. For a moment, Estella didn't recognize it, as it was genuine and held actual warmth. "I just adore you. Can't you see from everything you've become, you're mine?"

Jasper's pleas for her not to become the Baroness echoed in Estella's ears. He had said the very opposite: that she was better and stronger and kinder than the Baroness. Was he wrong? "You left me to die," Estella said, hating the emotion that had slipped into her voice.

"A mistake," the Baroness said. "And one we can get past. I know it."

"I disagree," Estella said.

But the Baroness didn't buy it. "You're not here for revenge," she said. Estella started to protest, but the Baroness stopped her. "You're here because you're a brilliant designer and a wicked genius, and so you need to be around your kind. Me."

Estella let her shoulders fall slightly. "We are very alike, I suppose," she admitted.

"Exactly," the Baroness said, happy to have gotten through to the girl. "Peas in a pod. Nothing to be ashamed of, Cruella. That's who you are. People like us make a drab world exceptional. That's why they hate us." Estella pretended to soften, and the Baroness pushed on. "So who else understands you? Me. Your *real* mother. Who made a mistake and let something extraordinary go." She paused and then said softly, "I'm sorry."

Estella had spent so long planning for this moment that she hadn't actually taken the time to think about what the moment would actually look like. And standing here now, on the cliffside where everything had started years ago, seeing what appeared to be genuine sympathy on the Baroness's face, she felt a whirl of emotions. She had anticipated feeling angry. She had *not* anticipated feeling sad. Estella shook her head. She didn't care what the Baroness said. The woman was a pro at working a room and a runway. Estella wouldn't let her work *her*. She knew better than to believe anything the woman said.

"Can I hug you?" the Baroness asked, holding out her arms.

Estella pretended to hesitate. This request was going to make things so much easier. "You're not going to throw me off the cliff, are you?"

"You're so funny, my darling," the Baroness said, smiling warmly. "I love it." Wrapping her arms around her, she squeezed Estella tightly. Then the squeeze grew uncomfortably tight. In her arms, Estella struggled to breathe. The Baroness turned her head and whispered into her ear. "Idiot," she said–just as she shoved her backward.

Estella only had time to shout in surprise and hear the telltale pop of a camera flash before she disappeared over the side of the cliff and plummeted toward the beach below.

Chapter 26

Time seemed to slow as Estella fell back through the misty air. She wondered, vaguely and with some distance, whether this was how her mother had felt when she fell from the same spot. But the thought was fleeting.

No sooner had she vanished from view than Estella raised her arms and her cape snapped open. The Estella outfit was frumpy for a reason: it was hiding the corset and extra fabric she had sewn inside. As the air whooshed through her ears, she pulled a string. The extra fabric billowed out above her, forming a handmade parachute. Catching and filling with air, she jerked up as her momentum slowed. Then, ever so slowly, she hit the water, barely making a splash.

Horace rowed over in a small dinghy. "There she is," he said, happy to see his friend.

She held up a hand as she treaded water. "Little help?"

Hauling her up over the side of the boat, Horace handed Estella a towel. She quickly dried herself off, and as Horace rowed them back to shore, she completed her final costume change for the evening.

She had a small window of time to complete her plan. As soon as the boat touched sand, Estella and Horace made their way to the waiting DeVille. She put the final touches on her makeup as he drove her up a narrow path and parked the car a short distance from where the Baroness still stood.

Only now she wasn't alone. She was surrounded by curious partygoers, bodyguards, and a handful of police. She was gesturing wildly to the cliff. "She jumped!" Estella heard her say. "She wanted to kill me, and she tried to take me with her . . ." Her voice trailed off as the police commissioner appeared, cuffs in hand.

Hidden in the darkness, Estella watched, a smile on her face as the commissioner stopped in front of the Baroness. She started to repeat her claim, but the man shook his head. He had been here before. And while that first time he had been young and naive and awed by the Baroness's wealth and power, this time he was not. He had gotten a report of a burglary at Hellman Hall and a pile of evidence showing just how many bad things the Baroness had done over the years.

The police commissioner wrenched the Baroness's arms behind her back, slapped the cuffs around her wrists, and led her toward the waiting police van. Guests lined up, watching with mouths agape, while Anita clicked her camera furiously. It was a train wreck, and no one wanted to look away.

"Can't you idiots see this was all a trick!" the Baroness was saying, still clinging to the foolish hope that she could get out of this one. "That Estella person *is* Cruella!"

Estella took a breath. That was her cue. From her spot, she spoke out. "Oh, Baroness," she said, enjoying the look of fear on the Baroness's face at the sound of her voice. Even in the dark, she could see the woman had paled. "It's Cruella De Vil."

Beside her, Horace couldn't help himself. "It's spelt like 'devil' but pronounced 'De Vil.'"

Giving her friend a smile, Estella stepped out of the shadows, her body illuminated from the headlights of the car, which Horace snapped on. She was dressed to kill–or be killed. Her outfit was glorious, the best thing she had ever created. Black, white, and tight, she looked like a predator. And her eyes were glued to her prey.

Moving forward, she cocked a hip and crossed her arms. She glanced around the crowd, seeing the shock on their faces, as though they truly thought she had risen from the grave.

"And I thought I was going to be fashionably late," Estella went on. She shook her head. "Now what are you blaming me for this time, Baroness? I certainly hope not that ensemble." She gestured to the Baroness's chain mail. She was enjoying pretending she hadn't been there the entire time.

The police commissioner looked back and forth

between the two women. Then he shook his head. "Ms. De Vil," he said. "We thought you were dead."

"Yes, I noticed," she said in her thick Cruella accent. "I go on a buying trip to Paris, I come home and everyone thinks I'm deceased." She shot the Baroness a look as she added, "Wishful thinking?"

She was still shaking her head as the Baroness was shoved–rather roughly–into the police van. Just as the doors clanged shut, the Baroness let out a cry of rage. "You wait!" she screamed. "I'll get even!"

"Ohh!" Estella said in mock fright. "I'm shaking."

But she wasn't shaking. Far from it. For the first time in a long while, Estella felt steady. She looked around at her friends who had gathered in the front of the crowd of women dressed as her. Jasper, Horace, Artie, John, Anita, even the Dalmatians–they were all there. For her. And they always had been. They were her family.

She gave them a grateful smile as she turned and began to walk through the crowd back toward the mansion. They had done it. They had won. Her mother's death had been avenged. She had a whole new future ahead of her full of endless possibility and enormous wealth. She wasn't quite sure what that future would look like. Not yet, at least. But dealing with the Baroness had not just deepened her love of fashion–it had given her a thirst for power.

And she couldn't wait to quench it.

But there was one last thing she had to do before Cruella could take her place in Hellman Hall. She had one last goodbye to make.

Estella stood above a fresh grave, staring at the newly dug dirt. On the headstone was the name Estella, followed by *R.I.P.* In smaller letters were the words *designer, daughter,* and *dead.*

Clutching her mother's necklace in her hands, Estella stared at the words, letting them sink in. She had been all those things. She had been a designer–not only creating incredible fashions but fashioning a new life for herself, designing the plan that ultimately got rid of the Baroness. And she had been a daughter–a true one to the woman, Catherine, whom she would always think of as her real mum, a stand-in for a woman who was incapable of love.

She looked at John. His face was sad and still as he stared at the grave. In a way, she realized, she was still a daughter. And a sister, and a friend, she added as her gaze landed on Horace, Jasper, and Anita.

But of all the words, the one that was most true now was *dead*. For Estella had died. She had been dying for years. Bit by bit. First the ginger boy had taken some of her; then her mum's death and the years on the street had followed. It would have been easy to say that the Baroness was the "murderer", but Estella knew the truth. Estella had been destined to fade away for a long time. In the hard world, there wasn't room for her gentle kindness or big heart. The Baroness had taught her that. If she was going to succeed–and she very much wanted to succeed–she was going to have to put that part of her in the ground forever. She was never going to let anyone walk all over her the way the Baroness had, and she wasn't going to let anyone ever see her weaknesses.

She shook her head and took a breath. It was time to get this over with. Letting the necklace dangle between her fingers, she began her own eulogy. "A nice girl, quiet, sweet . . . but a little bit boring and a tiny bit scared.

Trapped by her past, unsure of the future. Murdered tragically." She paused to see if the others would argue. When they didn't, she went on. "There was only one person who loved her, and loved her so dearly, and they're together now." This time, she saw Jasper shift on his feet and open his mouth to say something, but she pushed on, not letting him. She didn't want to hear him say she was loved. She didn't have time for that . . . not now. "Goodbye, Estella," she said, tossing the necklace into the grave. Then she wiped her hands. "All right, we should play a song or something to lighten the mood."

On the other side of the grave, Horace blew his nose loudly. "She's not actually dead, mate," Jasper pointed out.

Horace looked surprised by his friend's cool tone. "You didn't get caught up in all that?" he said. "You must be made of stone."

Jasper shrugged and started away from the grave. Estella, now Cruella, watched him go, taking the last of her innocence with him. Jasper had always been her voice of reason, her guidepost. But she was not the same girl anymore. She was moving on to the next stage of her life. From now on, Cruella would be the only voice in her head.

Jasper was going to have to grow a hard skin if he was going to stay in her life.

With one last look at the grave, Cruella followed Jasper out of the cemetery and into the waiting DeVille. The time for saying goodbyes and thinking about the past was over. She looked ahead, her eyes on the road. She had things to do—a brand to build, a mansion to move into.

Careering through the gates of Hellman Hall, she turned the radio up as the tires spun, shooting gravel. Suddenly, she slammed on the brakes. She jumped out, opened the trunk, and pulled out a crowbar. As the sun set, she walked to the sign attached to the gates. *Hellman Hall* was written in ornate letters that glowed in the golden light. She shook her head. Hellman Hall had been the Baroness's home. She leaned forward, digging the crowbar into the first word. Behind her Horace whooped as *man* came off the sign.

Cruella took a step back and looked at the new name: Hell Hall. *Yes,* she thought, *that is much better.* She got into the car and drove the rest of the way, humming a song to herself as the mansion, lit from within, came into view.

Inside, John would be waiting, a fire would be lit, and

the dogs would be chewing their bones. Let people believe that she was scary, that she could take down the Baroness. Let them see her and get a chill. The Baroness had once told her that to win, you had to be the first one to fight.

"So what now?" Jasper asked as they walked through the door and entered their new home.

Cruella stopped, grabbing a pencil and pad from a table. Putting the pencil to her bright red lips, she pursed them and smiled. "I've got a few ideas," she said, and with a flick of her signature hair, she stalked off, disappearing into the mansion.

She was ready to jump in the fight. Taking down the Baroness had been just the beginning. When she was done, the town, the whole city, maybe even the world would be seeing in black and white.